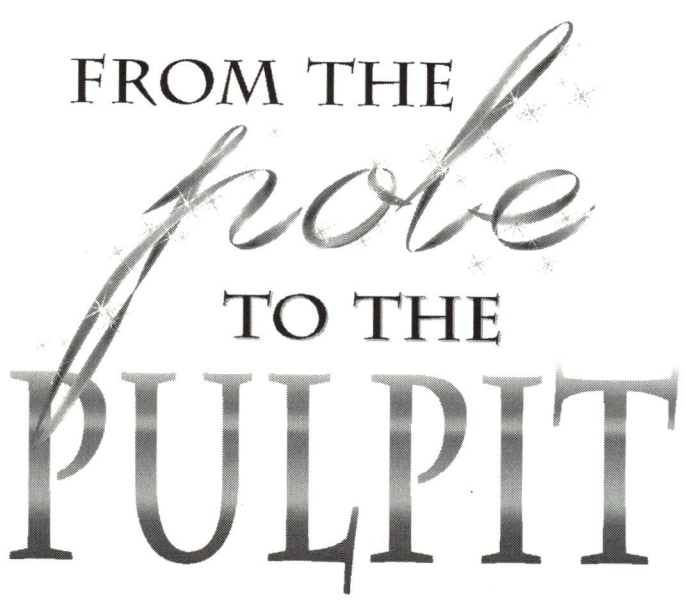

FROM THE pole TO THE PULPIT

EDQUINA WASHINGTON

EDQUINA WASHINGTON

motique media

Publishing division of Motique Momentums, LLC

www.danielaGabrielle.com/aspiring-authors

Copyright © 2014 Edquina Washington

All rights reserved.

ISBN:0692285539
ISBN-13:9780692285534

For Davina

TABLE OF CONTENTS

	Acknowledgments	vi
	Introduction	xi
1	From The Pole	1
2	The Sunshine After The Clouds	19
3	When It Rains…It Pours	29
4	The Truth Shall Set Us Free	41
5	New Beginnings and Old Endings	59
6	Secrets Bear Spoiled Fruits	77
7	Can We Say "Chuuuuuuuuuuuuuuuurch	89
8	Opportunities Knock	109
9	Nothing Is Constant But Change	127
10	No Drama, Like Church Drama	147
11	HE Works In Mysterious Ways	161
12	To The Pulpit	177

ACKNOWLEDGMENTS

I'm eternally grateful to the presence and saving grace of Jesus Christ in my life. My gifts, talents, joys, peace, and belonging are all because of HIM and the work that HE continues to do in my life.

To my Grandparents, Mr. James "Nat" Washington & Mrs. Dorothy "Dot" Washington, you will forever be missed. Your memories and timeless guidance will forever be at the forefront of my days and nights. There is not a day that goes by that I do not think of the both of you and the impact that you have had in my life. I LOVE YOU and I am blessed to have had the chance to call the both of you Grand pop and Grand mom.

Thank you to my Mother for raising me to be the strong – willed and independent woman that I am. I LOVE YOU for all that you do for me and my babies. To my family, which this entire book would take up mentioning each and every one of them, your support and love is always appreciated. Aunt G, I LOVE YOU and THANK YOU for always supporting me in every single thing that I've ever done.

To my crew, Shane, Coco, Co-Trika, Liz, Tanisha, Lizette, and Jamiel, your ears, eyes, time, support, laughter and love throughout this process has meant so very much to me. To my friend from way back when, Tesha, LOVE YOU. It is always a blessing to have friends that have actually become your family.

Daniela, thank you for pushing me, motivating me, and believing in me throughout this entire project. Your inspiration is truly admirable and it was an honor to work with you.

Davina, **I LOVE YOU**. You wanted this, so here it is. You believed that if you gave the title, I could write it and you were right. I couldn't ask for a better Sister!

To everyone that has ever believed in me,

offered me a kind word, a mean word, a hug, a roll of their eyes, or a smile. THANK YOU. I appreciate you and your presence in my life.

As women, we must stop holding back our stories of triumph and sadness and share them. Every woman has a story, so why not share it, to help the next woman understand that it's okay to struggle, fight, stand up, be knocked down, and stand back up again.

"The day that we as women discontinue judging one another, will be the day that we PERSEVERE."

EDQUINA WASHINGTON

INTRODUCTION

Bold and fierce
Cocoa skin that could rage a war
Nubian fire
Bet I could light your flame
Sculptured structure
Perfect waist for holding
Perfect ways for knowin
I can drop that
Pop that
Slide that
Let you smack that
Flip that
Rub it down
Ohhhhhhhhhhh Nooooo…..
Maybe a Mystery
For the right price, with the bat of my eyes I lost my soul
Somewhere between the rush of fortune and the stupidity of pride
Standing on the stage of my demise
Sharing my spirit with perfect strangers
Chemically unbalancing my entire being
Pretending that the character of my heart's exterior was never given to me
Soiled demons reap at my existence
Planting their feet around my solid ground
Chains imaginary but as real as can be
Until HE spoke to me
Un-plain as a midnight day
In the mirror of confusion and the pit of nothingness
HE spoke to ME
In my 6 inch heels
Holding onto my insatiable sin
Back up against the wall, but facing the ceiling
Dropping to my knees
Naked, but feeling clothed for once
Wholeness welcoming me at its front door
With a universal key
Dancing across it's threshold for HIS name
Chanting in psalm
HE gave me some free
HE gave me some free
It was MY GOD that gave me some FREE

Morgan

EDQUINA WASHINGTON

Chapter 1
FROM THE POLE

"It is in the shadows of our sins that we often find our faith"

"Ughhh another worthless date," uttered Morgan. "He was a complete waste of my time, I could have been somewhere else doing something else well worth my time," she thought to herself. This dating mess, is not for me. "Men are so damn lame nowadays," Morgan whispered to herself as she pulled out her MAC compact to touch up her makeup. "I need to hit up the mall before I go to work tonight, so I gotta make this quick," she thought to herself. As she opened her car and slid down in her leather seats, she let a calming sigh out, feeling that she could finally breathe. It has always been like this for her; go on a date and the only thing that her date would do is stare at her body like she's a piece of meat or compliment her on it for the entire date, as if she didn't hear that two thousand times a day. "I mys well give up," she muffled under her breathe. She started her car and made her way to Towers Mall. When she arrived, she put in her ear buds and took a long breathe as Sade made love to her ears.

As she made her way to Nordstrom's, she thought about wanting something more in life than what she had. Yes, it was a blessing to wake up and have the ability to buy any of the designer clothes and top of the line home furnishings she desired, but at what cost? An empty home? An empty heart? "Whatever," blurted out Morgan. "Excuse me, how may I help you," asked the clerk. Morgan smiled uncomfortably, "Sorry about that, I was thinking about something else, can I see those shoes in a 9 ½ please?"

After leaving the mall, all Morgan could think about was not being late tonight. For the past few months, deep down inside she had been feeling as if her world was crashing down on her and that there had to be something more to life than dancing, but it's all that she had and all that she knew, other than hustlin'…and that was not an option.

Her feelings were causing her to care less and less about working. She just didn't have the energy anymore or the thrill of dancing that she once had years ago. At one time, it was something fun to do that was an easy way to make money. Now, more and more, she began to think about how disgusting she felt parading around in her nude and allowing the most perverted type of men touch all over her body.

At what price was that worth? The looks on their faces just disgusted her these days. "Ahhhhhhh……Where am I going!!!!" yelled Morgan at the top of her lungs, as she fell back on her bed full of pillows. She closed her eyes and stared at the ceiling as tears rolled down the side of her face. Morgan knew that things had to change, but she also knew that today, was just not the day.

"Here we go," Morgan whispered to herself as she ran out of her car and into work twenty – two minutes late. She opened up the rear door and tried her best to hurry past *Fat Kat* and run to her locker, but she was caught. "Mystery, how many times do I have to tell you to stop comin' up in here late." "Come in here late one more time and your old ass is out the door." "You better act like you know, cuz don't nobody else up or down the east coast want your old ass slidin' down their pole," yelled *Fat Kat*. Morgan just laughed, along with the other girls Sugar and Lace. She knew deep down inside that Fat Kat was serious, but tried her best not to show it. It was only a matter of time, but that would be an obstacle that she would face when it presented itself.

The locker room was just that, a locker room that smelled like a little bit of this and a little bit of that; body oils, perfume, coochie, and dirty clothes. The environment was loud and catty, with the aesthetics of a high school locker room, locker stickers, female drama, fights and all. Morgan sat on the cold wooden bench, opened her locker and started to transform herself into Mystery. Thirty-minutes later and she was ready to go; full coverage makeup, seven inch heels, barely there outfit, flowing black hair and mind on her money.

It was Mystery's time to grace the stage of club *Top Shelf*. Mystery was always a show stopper. For her age, she had a body that all the other dancers hated and all of the men wanted to touch; full chest, tiny waist, sensual hips, thighs and a behind that forced everyone to look. Her skin was like chocolate silk; no tattoos and no embellishments. Her long jet black hair cascaded down her back like a never ending wave. Morgan had eyes that left you wondering; and that's why Fat Kat named her Mystery. Unlike the other women that aged with time, as she got older, she seemed to blossom. She was his money maker and truth be told, that's why he kept her around. He would never risk letting her go.

Morgan was ready to get her money and call it a night. She wiped down her pole and could see that it was a full house in Top Shelf. Once she heard her song, she knew that it was show time. The pole was her best friend. She worked hard at mastering her craft; to the point that a blind man could tell that she worked it. The night seemed to be going well, not to mention that her stage was flooded with dough. Morgan grabbed up her money and made her way to the back. She only had a few minutes to stash her cash, refresh, and change her gear to make her way on the floor for lap dances. Walking through the room like a prize, at one time empowered her, but now it was becoming one of the most nauseating parts of her job. She had her regulars that got off on a variety of things from rubbin' her ass, her chest, grinding in their laps, or simply listening to their issues with their wives. It was like she was a nude therapist.

Morgan made her way over to a customer, collected her cash, and began grinding on him, when he suddenly turned her around and had his hands in her ass. She tried to get away, but she couldn't, the grip that he had on her was too strong. "You like that don't you," he whispered to her. Morgan was completely disgusted. As she started to kick the guy in his balls, Lance from security grabbed him up and took him out the spot. Morgan fixed herself back up in the matter of seconds and went onto the next one. This was a daily routine, there was always one that would go too far and you just had to expect it and move on. She had worked all shifts, but preferred night shift, because at that time, the money was right.

Morgan finished her shift and made her way to the locker room when she ran into Lance. "Damn Lance, where were you, he could've really hurt me," Morgan yelled. I got'um didn't I, I'm not the only one workin' the floor tonight," replied Lance. "Yeah you're right, whatever, thanks anyway," Morgan said nonchalantly to Lance, knowing that security could've gotten to her sooner. Sometimes, she would think that security was in cahoots with customers and received the same amount of satisfaction watching them in distress as the customers got. She kept thinking, "why in the hell do I keep putting up with this....this is bull shit. Morgan was a veteran at Top Shelf and that meant she got preference over a lot, including her schedule. She had been dancing there since she was seventeen. She's seen plenty come and plenty go in her eleven years. She's seen it all and experienced it all; almost beat to death, raped too many times to count, dabbled in coke and enjoyed alcohol and weed, stalked by regulars, entertained threesomes and foursomes, and still lonely as hell!

Just thinking about it all, gave her the

worst feeling in the world. Morgan pulled out her flask and began to drown herself in liquid happiness. She sat down on the wooden bench and began to allow the euphoric intoxication to take over her being. A few of the ladies began to make their way back into the locker room, when Morgan seen her homegirl Sugar walk by. Sugar was a few years younger than Morgan, but had only been dancing at Top Shelf for the past 3 years. Morgan kind of took Sugar under her wings, when she first came into Top Shelf. She knew firsthand how ignorant and rude the other dancers could treat newbies and there was something sweet about Sugar's spirit that Morgan liked.

Sugar wasn't as rough around the edges as most of the other dancers that made their way through the doors of Top Shelf and Morgan made it her mission to teach her the ropes.

"Sugar, how was your night Boo," Morgan asked. "Aiight," she answered, as she made her way towards her locker. "How bout you?" she asked Mystery. "Same drama, different day......but we gotta eat somehow," commented Morgan. "Ain't that the truth, Sis," agreed Sugar. Morgan pulled up an old rusty metal chair, close to the bench, and propped her feet right on it. Her ankles and the soles of her feet hurt like nobody's business. Parading around in seven inch heels and making someone else's fantasy come true for the night, was without a doubt hard work and the throbbing pain of Morgan's ankles and feet, were without a doubt physical proof of that. She slowly relaxed her body forward, while rubbing her ankles, hoping to erase the pain that she felt, in both her soles and soul.

Morgan was tired of being Mystery, but really didn't know how to be anyone else. She allowed her thoughts to take over her mind, as they danced slowly from memory to memory of the fun she had with her best friend LaKeya and brother Maurice, when she was younger. The laughter, the smiles, and pure innocence of joy suddenly overcame her and she began to silently cry. With her face unexposed and pressed against her chocolate limbs, Morgan could feel the wetness of her tears resting upon her legs. As she lifted her head, she could hear that remaining dancers make their way into the back room. She started to wipe the tears from her legs and ripped off a few pieces of toilet paper that was resting on the mirror stand to blot under her eye.

Unknowingly to the other dancers, Morgan watched as they made their way towards the bathroom and lockers and allowed their conversation to filter through her mind, not actually listening to them, but allowing their voices to take precedence over the numbing silence that she was feeling in her spirit. She thought to herself, "if only they knew that some days around here are a nightmare, others are as mundane as the seconds passing by, and that good days will never be remembered, they would run realizing that nothing was Top Shelf about this place or this life." "But hey, who am I to judge, when I'm sitting here right along with them, doing the same damn thing and for the longest amount of time," she thought to herself.

Morgan had spent the majority of her adulthood morphing herself into this persona, not realizing that it would become extremely difficult to picture herself as anyone or anything else. In the fog of her mind, while getting dressed and ready to leave for the night, Morgan overheard Lace and Fat Kat talking in his office. She couldn't make out everything that they were saying, but she knew that she heard Lace say her name. Morgan was furious. Her ears were on fire, her heart was pounding and she wanted to know why her name was flying out of Lace and Fat Kat's mouth. She waited patiently by the edge of the second row of lockers, until Lace walked by. Just as Lace was walking by, Morgan grabbed Lace by the back of the neck and dropped her to floor. "Why the hell you got my name in your mouth Lace?" "You got a problem with me?" yelled Morgan. Lace was trying her best to get Morgan off of her, but it wasn't working. She tried screaming, but nothing was coming out, Morgan had her. "Keep my name outta your mouth," demanded Morgan. "Morgan get off of her," yelled Sugar.

Sugar tried to get Morgan's arm from around Lace's neck, but she couldn't. Morgan realized what she was doing, turned around and could see the other dancers standing around her and looking. She immediately dropped Lace to the floor, made her way back to her locker, pulled out her Louis Vuitton bag, walked out the door, got in her ride and drove off. "I'm tired of this shit!" "Fuck!" She screamed at the top of her lungs. Her heart hurt, her spirit was broke, and she felt lost. She knew it was wrong that she chocked Lace up like that, but she had it coming anyhow.

If there's one unspoken rule at Top Shelf, it's don't fuck with Mystery, and Lace's stupid ass broke that. There was a façade that Morgan had to uphold and keep while she was in Top Shelf and she was not about to allow anyone or anything up in there take that from her. Morgan knew she had to get herself back together, so she did the only thing that could calm her down. She opened her console, pulled out her L, lifted the volume on Sade coming through the speakers, and smoked herself into ecstasy. Yesssss…she sang, as Sade's "No Ordinary Love" blared, "This…is…no ordinary love…no ordinary love." There was just something about that song and her L that put her at ease. She couldn't explain it, but knew it was her antidote to drama, which for some reason was happening just about every damn day at Top Shelf. Buzzz….Buzzz, Morgan felt her phone vibrating and knew who it was, Fat Kat. She looked at the phone in disgust, knowing that, she would have to go back to hell and deal with the devil for at least a few more hours.

As she pulled back into the parking lot, she saw Fat Kat outside waiting for her. Morgan rolled her eyes. She tried to slide past Fat Kat on the step, she grabbed the handle of the door and tried to open it, but he pushed it back shut.

"C'mon Fatz, stop playing games and let me in," hissed Morgan. Fat Kat gave Morgan a cold hard look in the eyes and released the door. Morgan walked in the door and mumbled under her breath, "Asshole." As she passed Lace and some of the other girls passing by and making their way back out to the floor, everything got quiet. Yeah, don't play with me again, she thought to herself. "You good Boo?" questioned Sugar. "Cool as a fan Ma…Cool as a fan," Morgan answered. "It's always the one that thinks they need to prove a point around here that will end up kissing this dirty ass floor," commented Morgan confidently.

Morgan ended her last lap dance for the night, was walking into the back, when she caught the eye of a customer staring at her. She gave a seductive wink and it appeared that the guy mouthed "Morgan." She looked back and quickly ran into the back room. Morgan peeked back through the curtain separating the backroom from the showroom floor, so he couldn't see that she was taking another look, but could not place the face of the guy. Nothing about him stuck out at all. "Maybe, I'm trippin," she whispered to herself. But I was sure his lips said "Morgan." "Maybe somebody from school or something…wouldn't be the first time that that has happened," she thought to herself. Morgan pulled out her flask and allowed its contents to warm her throat and body, got dressed, and flew out the door. She couldn't leave Top Shelf fast enough. Every year, every day, and every second was getting worse and the most depressing. The truth about the situation was that she had no choice, but to stay and endure the pain. Well, at least, that's what she thought.

Chapter 2
THE SUNSHINE AFTER THE CLOUDS

Bzzzz...Bzzzz....Bzzz.... Morgan looked at the phone and seen it was her girl Lakeya calling. "Hey Boo what's up," answered Morgan. "Just wanted to check on you and see if you remembered that Joy's 5th birthday party was today at five." "She would love to see you there, you know you're her favorite Auntie," joked Lakeya. Morgan smiled, "of course, I wouldn't miss it for anything." Morgan and Lakeya were friends from way back to Salvation Army camp days. They never went to the same school, but always managed to keep in touch over the years. Lakeya had all of the things that Morgan so desperately wanted: happiness, a home, a husband, a family, a career, and love. Morgan and Lakeya may have chosen different walks of life, but in all reality they were the same. They came from the same town, on the same street, but with a different story. When they were together, they were the same teenage girls that would sit together on the bus every day to Salvation Army camp and gossip about everyone and everything.

Morgan loved Lakeya and her family. She felt as if they were the only piece of normality that she had in her life and often suffocated herself in their world, especially when the inconsistencies in her life were too much to bear. Lakeya loved Morgan all the same, even though her husband Damian didn't care much that her best friend was a career stripper. Morgan was the sister that she never had and she would never turn her back on her. Lakeya understood the heart that Morgan had and prayed that one day, she would reach her true destiny in life. She would never leave Morgan's side and that was a vow they took way back in the day.

Morgan was excited every time that she got the chance to shop for Joy. She desperately wanted a child, but knew that she lived a life that would not be in the best interest of a child. Everything in the store, seemed perfect for Joy. Although Morgan wanted to buy the entire store, she settled on a few gifts that she knew for sure would make Joy the happiest little girl in the world.

As soon as she stepped out of the store, Morgan realized where she knew that guy she'd seen at work last week, it was Troy, LaKeya's husband's friend that she met a few years ago at a cookout. Morgan just smirked and thought to herself about how much she sees men that sneak and drive an entire hour away to indulge in their secrets hoping to not get caught. She assumed that Troy was one of them. Morgan knew for sure that if he and his wife were going to be at the birthday party, Troy would find a way to corner her and ask her to keep his little secret and she was going to take advantage of that opportunity if it presented itself. "Dummy," she whispered as she got into her car.

It was a hot and sticky August day. As soon as Morgan got into her house, she flopped on the couch and took in all the central air that she could. "What am I going to wear," she mumbled. Morgan wanted to call LaKeya to chat it up before the birthday party about seeing Troy's skeemin' ass at *Top Shelf* and how surprised he was to see her there that he was mouthing her name, but she knew that Lakeya was getting everything perfect for Joy's party and didn't want to disturb her, so she would wait to spill the beans at the party while they were off chillin'.

LaKeya pulled all her skills out the bag to decorate Joy's party. She really made the room look like a princess palace, everything was perfect, even the cake. As soon as Morgan walked through the door, Joy ran up to her yelling "Auntie Morgan's here," while giving her a big hug. Morgan just stood there staring a Joy running away with her gift thinking how she once felt that way; happy and carefree without a worry. It's been a long time for that, she thought to herself.

While they were cleaning up, Morgan couldn't resist filling LaKeya in on the details of Troy. "I can believe it," stated LaKeya. "He and his wife have been having issues with him and several women." "He thought that he could keep his devilish ways a secret, but we all know that what you do in dark always comes to the light," explained LaKeya. "Can we get an AMEN," joked Morgan. "Yeah, I was excited, thinking that I was gonna see him here today; I was ready to offer several opportunities to sporadically forget his little secret," stated Morgan.

"You need to stop doing that stuff Morg, you know no good comes outta that," exclaimed LaKeya. "Well, it does plenty of good for my bills and necessities, I don't know what you're talkin' bout!" stated Morgan as she stood up and struck a pose. They both started to laugh uncontrollably, to the point that Damian came in the room, looked at them and just shook his head. "If only he knew," whispered Morgan. Damian enjoyed seeing LaKeya happy and laughing, but was often on the fence about her and Morgan hanging out. Damian knew that

LaKeya was her own woman, but he also knew that for her and Morgan to have the bond that they have, that there most definitely had to be some commonalities between them both. Of the five years that he and LaKeya had been married, Damian hadn't felt this unsure about his relationship with LaKeya. Things have just not been the same and Damian could not put his finger on it. He knew that marriage wasn't always to be about bliss, but he also knew that when his gut was telling him something, he'd better take notice to it.

LaKeya walked Morgan to the door, when Joy came running up to them, hugging Morgan on her legs. "Don't leave Auntie Morgan, I want to show you something," pleaded Joy. "You can show me next time sweetie, your Mommy said it's time for bed," explained Morgan. Joy became visibly upset and began to cry. "Okay, you can show me really quick," whispered Morgan playfully. Joy grabbed her hand and took off racing up the stairs to her bedroom. Joy was so excited to show Morgan her new doll house that she could hardly speak without giggling with excitement. LaKeya stood in the middle of the foyer, shaking her head. "C'mon Joy, Auntie Morgan has to go home and you need to go to bed," calmly yelled LaKeya up the stairs. "We can play with your baby dolls next time Joy, okay?" questioned Morgan. "Okay, I never have anybody to play with," expressed Morgan. "I pinky promise that we will play next time that I come over," explained Morgan. Joy had a huge smile across her face, threw her arms in the air and yelled, "Yaaaaaaaaaaaaaaaaaaaaaayyy….. I can't wait." Morgan simply hugged Joy and treaded lightly down the stairs. She hugged and kissed LaKeya goodbye and yelled goodbye to Damian.

Morgan walked to her car grinning and feeling happy, from the wonderful time that she had at Joy's birthday party. She thought the world of LaKeya, Damian, and Joy and thought that they were the real life Cosby family, minus the excess of children.

EDQUINA WASHINGTON

Chapter 3
WHEN IT RAINS...IT POURS

Unfortunately, it was about that time to walk into the wonderful wild world of *Top Shelf*. Morgan grabbed her stuff out of the car and opened the door to her hell. Everything was everything and business was as usual in Top Shelf for a Wednesday night. When she got back to her area, she noticed that the lock on her locker had been tampered with. She looked around the room and no one was in sight. Everyone was out on the floor and the main person that she suspected was that new chick Lace, but she knew that around there, it could just be about anyone.

"Fatz, who was tryna get in my locker," questioned Morgan. "How the hell do I know, I ain't your damn keeper," blurted Fat Kat. "Maybe if you stop being such a bitch and beatin' people's asses around here, then maybe you wouldn't have these type of problems," stated Fat Kat. "Shut the fuck up Fatz, I don't even know why the hell I wasted my time asking you," yelled Morgan as she slammed his door and walked out.

Morgan could not remember the last time that she felt safe. The last time that she felt as if she didn't have to keep looking over her shoulder in wait of the next big drama saga to continue throughout her life. "Something has got to give…..I'm all tapped out and I'm gettin' too old for this." "I'm gonna either end up dead or locked the fuck up for killin' one of these young girls," she thought. "Marsala, bring me two of my usual so I can get ready for the night," cuz it looks like it's gonna be a long one tonight, she boasted.

"There ain't no damn money out there," shouted Sharifa. "You right about that, I think I'm gonna leave early up outta here, cuz it's real dry on the floor," stated Lace as she gave Sharifa a high five. "I got some business we can take care of together later, if you're game," stated Lace. Morgan rolled her eyes and continued to look for her makeup as her back was turned to them. She thought, "These young girls are slow," as she shook her head. Morgan knew all too well, where being thirsty for money had led her and it was sad that these young girls had no idea. It's crazy how fast they come through these revolving doors and end up turning the key to a lock too easy to open and hard as a rock to close.

The floor was right, the night was good and it felt like every dollar ever owned by a man was Morgan's. She finished her act, snatched up her bills and stepped into the lounge area with a smirk on her face. Morgan knew that those young girls had no idea what they were talking about. For the life of them, they could not understand that they must work for the money and that it wasn't just going to come to them because they had a fat ass, huge breasts and a tiny waist. Making the decision to become a stripper wasn't one that Morgan was forced into, it was a decision that she made. Morgan knew that every day she stepped foot into *Top Shelf* that it was not going to be a good feeling and that was the main thing that was eating at her for the past few months. She wanted something new, something fresh, and something that made her feel as if she had worth, but she had no idea how to reach it, where it was at, and if she even had the stamina and courage to explore what was creeping up inside of her every day.

Morgan changed into her clothes, walked

out the door, and began to breathe a breath of relief. Ughhhh, it was so Hot!!! The air in the car couldn't cool her leather seats off fast enough. As she got in her car and pulled her phone out of her console, she noticed that she had 5 missed calls from LaKeya. "Shit," screamed Morgan. Several thoughts ran through her head in the matter of seconds, as she called LaKeya back. "Keya is everything okay?" exclaimed Morgan. "Morg no it's not, where are you?" asked LaKeya. "In my car, why, what is it, stop playin' games with me," stated Morgan. "It's your brother, Maurice, Morg he's been shot & he needs you...do you need me to come get you?" questioned LaKeya "No, I'm there," cried Morgan. "I'll be in the front waiting for you, I got you," whispered LaKeya. Morgan broke down and cried like she never cried before. She felt as if a ton of bricks had fell on top of her and she couldn't move. She didn't have anything to smoke or nothin' to drink to numb the pain that she was feeling. She looked up to the roof of her car and whispered, "God just help me get there!"

Thoughts of her brother and their last conversation circled through her mind like a song on repeat. Although there was silence in her car, she couldn't wait to get to the hospital and be with her brother to block out the loudness of her depressing thoughts. "Please let him live, just please let him live, I will give anything if he lives," she cried as she exited her car. Her feet couldn't move fast enough, she felt as if she was in a dream and her body was afloat in mid-air. As she approached the doors of the hospital, LaKeya was there waiting for her, but Morgan did not like the look on her face. "Morgan...," LaKeya yelled, as LaKeya grabbed her arm and continued to walk. "Where is he?" "What are they saying?" "Who did this to him?" shrieked

Morgan. "Just go see your brother Boo, don't worry about that now," guided LaKeya.

Walking through the curtain, all that she heard was beeping sounds and all that she seen was her brother laying there, lifeless and motionless, looking nothing like the brother that she knew. His face was swollen, tubes were running through him and it appeared as if every machine in the hospital was hooked up to him. She stood by his bed, grabbed his hand and kissed it. "You gonna make it through this, I don't care what I have to do" she whispered as tears raced down her cheek. LaKeya came up behind Morgan and rubbed her back softly. "Boo, the doctor wants to talk with you."

The pain had become unbearable, as Morgan thought about all the comments the doctor made about her brother's possibility of life being slim and the definite health concerns he would have, if he were to survive. "Who did this to you Maurice?" "Who would want to hurt him just enough to leave him almost dead?" she shrieked. He was stomped in the face and chest so many times, that he was just about unrecognizable. Police were coming in and out of the room, but Morgan said nothing to them and they said nothing to her. No condolences, no questions, no nothing. She hated that they treated her like she was invisible and like her brother's life was nothing more than another day on the beat.

"Oh shit, who are you?" Morgan yelled as she jumped up out of her chair. She didn't realize that it had been the next day. "Be easy, I'm Deuce, your brother was my mans." "If he was your mans so much, then why the hell is he layin' up in here?," hissed Morgan. "Yo, sweetheart, I'm sorry, I wasn't here, I feel bad as shit that he's up in here, trust me," explained Deuce. Morgan didn't like anything about Deuce, she never seen him before, never heard her brother talk about him, and needed to find out where the hell he came from. She kept her eyes on him as he walked around the bed. "How long did you know my brother and why I ain't never hear about you?," questioned Morgan. "I don't know anything about that, but here's where you can reach me if you need anything," stated Deuce as he handed his number to Morgan. She just looked at him, motionless, as he approached her with the slip of paper. "I'll just put it here on the table," Deuce whispered. Morgan watched as he walked out of the room and thought to herself, "I'm gonna find out about his ass tonight, if it's the last thing that I do!"

Morgan finally moved from her seated position and opened the curtains in the room.

"You need some sunshine," she stated as she made her way around the room to Maurice's bedside. "We're survivors and I'll be right here by your side until you are back to you" "These doctors don't know about the strength in our blood, we'll show them," Morgan expressed as tears formed in the corners of her eyes. In a hospital full of people she had never felt so alone. She hated the smell of the room, the looks on the faces of the doctors, how they spoke to her and the way her brother was lying there, lifeless and unaware.

Morgan allowed thought after thought to overcome her of every situation possible that she could have interjected to make this untrue, although she knew that none of it could change the situation. Her feelings became overwhelming and she could feel her knees buckle as she dropped to the floor calling on the name of

Jesus. Morgan felt as if something had taken over her body and was controlling her motions and the words coming out of her mouth. All that she felt were tears streaming down her face and she could hear uncommon words lifting from her tongue that left her with a euphoric feeling.

She had never, in her entire life recalled feeling this way before. As she arose from the floor, her hands were shaking. Morgan ran into the bathroom, closed the door, and stared into the mirror. She threw some water on her face, looked in the mirror again and just felt different. She couldn't explain it, but she knew for a fact that she felt different. Morgan opened the bathroom door, grabbed the piece of paper that Deuce left on the table and called Lakeya. Maurice was the only blood that she had left on earth and she knew she couldn't bear going on without him.

Chapter 4
THE TRUTH SHALL SET US FREE

"You ever hear of some dude named Deuce?" Morgan asked LaKeya as soon as she sat in the car. "No....Why should I'?" asked LaKeya. "Yeah, this guy showed up this morning in Maurice's room claiming to be his right hand, but I ain't never hear about'um," stated Morgan. "I'm gonna find out what his connection is to my brother and that's that," whispered Morgan as she glared out the car window. LaKeya thought it was weird as well that none of Maurice's boys came to see him or even called Morgan, but she kept her thoughts to herself. She could see that Morgan was emotionally and physically exhausted and left it for another day. Morgan knew that once she got home that she had to put word out on the streets to find out more about this Deuce guy and find out why none of her brother's clique came out to visit him at the hospital. Things just were not sitting right and she was determined to get down to the bottom of it all, if it was the last thing that she ever did.

As soon as she walked in the door, she screamed at the top of her lungs with all of her might. She took her hand and slapped the vases on her end table straight to the floor. She just wanted this to all end. She wanted everything to make sense and not have to search for missing pieces to this puzzle. Her head was throbbing so much and she just felt weak all over. Although Morgan wanted more than anything to go back out to the hospital with Maurice, she knew that she needed to get herself together, in order to be there fully for him.

Morgan got out of the shower and threw on some tights and a T-shirt. She proceeded to text one of her brothers' friends to find out what the hell was going on. Every five minutes she looked at her phone to check for a response, but there was none. It was burning her up inside. "What the hell is taking him so long," she muffled. She begin searching through all of her compartments and purses for something to relax her, but she couldn't find anything. Morgan, knew she had to have something in her house, but for some reason she couldn't find where she placed it at. She was becoming frustrated and just decided to pour herself a rum and coke and be done with it.

Morgan turned on the TV and flipped through the channels. Nothing on the screen could help ease her pain. She finally texted Fat Kat and let him know that she wouldn't be in for a while and would be in touch in a few days to let him know where she stood. Fat Kat called her back immediately, but she just let the phone ring. Morgan just didn't feel like explaining things to him and hearing him demand how he needed her at *Top Shelf*. In the back of her mind, Top Shelf was becoming a distraction, which had yet to play itself out in her life. She knew that if Fat Kat wanted to get her, he knew exactly where to find her. Morgan looked at her phone again to see if she had a message from her brother's friend Ty, but there was nothing, next thing she knew, she was asleep.

Once Morgan got up, she looked around and grabbed her phone. She noticed that she had a message from Ty and 5 voice mails from Fat Kat. Seriously, she giggled to herself, "Fatz has lost his mind! " Morgan couldn't wait to call Ty. "Ty, this is Morgan, we need to talk," she demanded. "Aiight, meet me at the diner on Delaney & Trust in a half, I'll be in the back," stated Ty. She hung up. Morgan got herself together and flew out the door. Her heart was racing so fast and her hands were shaking so much that she couldn't even turn the steering wheel. She was equally excited and afraid to hear what Ty had to say, but knew she had to know. Morgan took in a few deep breaths and whispered to herself, "You can do this!" She wanted to get to the diner before Ty, so that she could park and see him go in. Morgan wanted to make sure that Ty didn't beat her in the head and not show up. Low and behold, about seven minutes later, there he was. She pulled the mirror down in the car, checked her face, and flew out the car so fast, that she left her keys in the ignition. After running back across the street and grabbing her keys from the car, Morgan took in another deep breath, wiped the tears from her eyes as the voice inside said, "you can do this!"

"What's up Ty," grimaced Morgan. "You, baby girl," stated Ty. "Come on with all that Ty, look what's good?" "I don't have time for all of that." "I told you why I wanted to meet, so let's get down to it" demanded Morgan. "Aiight look, M is my man and everything, but he's into a whole 'nother world," explained Ty, while leading Morgan on. "And…." expressed Morgan! "What world is he into that you ain't have his back…..that's what I'm tryna understand" exclaimed Morgan. "Look baby girl, Deuce….that's your brother's man," Explained Ty. "Yeah, I can see, cuz he's the only one of y'all that showed my brother any kind of love," yelled Morgan. "Look, you need to calm down. You not gettin' what I'm trying to tell you….Deuce and your brother were together." "Maurice was gay sweetie and we all found out," whispered Ty. "What, so that that's why?" "That's why y'all weak asses left my brother for dead?" "So who did it...who did it Ty?" screamed Morgan as she slammed her hand down on the table. "Yo, calm your ass down," yelled Ty. "No, fuck you Ty!" "Fuck you and the entire ground that you and your crew walk on." "Stay the fuck away from me and mines," yelled Morgan. The entire diner was silenced, as Morgan and Ty were the main attraction. She grabbed her purse, flew open the door and ran to her car as tears bounced off her cheeks and into the passing wind. She started her car and sped off, leaving an everlasting tale of her frustration marked on Trust Street.

Thoughts were racing through her mind like the Indy five thousand. Maurice being gay, was just something that she couldn't believe. This had to be a rumor. It had to be an ugly rumor that spread to the streets before facts could be verified. She wanted to call LaKeya, but then she didn't want to call her. The thing that she wanted to do most, was find out who did this to Maurice and give it to them twenty two times worse!

Morgan couldn't get to her house fast enough, so that she could call Deuce and find out what the hell is going on. She called Deuce twice before he picked up. Morgan agreed to meet him in the hospital cafeteria. All of this was just too surreal. What if Maurice was really gay? Why didn't he tell me? Why did I have to find out this way? It had only been two days since the incident, but it felt like two years. She couldn't eat, she couldn't sleep right, or even think about working. Morgan felt as if her spirit would not rest until she got to the bottom of everything. Once she called LaKeya and filled her in on everything, she felt a bit calmer. Although LaKeya offered to go with her to meet with Deuce, Morgan turned the offer down. She just didn't want her to be involved at this point. Morgan didn't know how she would react and where she would end up as a result of her reaction, but she did know that she was ready to deal with any infraction for the love that she had for her brother.

As she entered the hospital room, she felt a sense of peace. The nurse came into the room after her and explained that Maurice had some great progress over the night and that they were expecting him to turn around. Morgan could not erase the huge smile that was plastered across her face. "Did you hear that Reece….you're gonna make it," she whispered in his ear. "You're a fighter and your little sisters' got everything under control, so don't worry," Morgan boasted. This was just the perfect way to start the day out, Morgan thought to herself. She went about her normal routine when coming to Maurice's hospital room; opening the blinds, fixing his covers, and talking to him about all the good times they had together growing up. She just wanted to keep everything about his room cheerful and lively, although the reality of the situation was the epitome of depression. Morgan grabbed one of Maurice's blankets and decided to relax for a bit. She could feel that she was extremely exhausted.

Morgan awoke to a knock at the door. She looked up and seen an older black woman standing at the door. "Good Morning Ma'am, may I pray with you for your loved one?" asked the woman. "Good Morning, who are you…who told you to come?" "I'm Chaplin Carrington, I visit daily with patients in the intensive care unit. I want to let you know that your loved one and your family are in our prayers, but what I really came for today was to pray with you," explained Chaplin Carrington. "Sure," stated Morgan. She placed her right hand in the outstretched hand of Chaplin Carrington and her left hand on Maurice and allowed the calmness of Chaplin Carrington's voice soothe her spirit and her soul. Morgan heard the words that she was speaking, but felt the power of the words. The words just took over her entirety and she just let the tears cascade down her face, not wiping them, just letting them release everything that was hurting her.

Everything that was nestled deep down inside of her appeared to surface with urgency. Morgan felt the warm hands of Chaplin Carrington hold her and rub her back. Chaplin Carrington whispered in Morgan's ear, "your truth is your triumph, God is with you my dear."

"Thank you," Morgan mouthed. "God Bless you my dear. You know where to find me if you need me. You and your family are in my prayers," stated Chaplin Carrington as she exited the room. Morgan wiped her tears, pulled her chair up next to her brother and laid her head on his bed. "I can't wait until you are out of here…," she whispered.

Morgan jumped up as she felt her phone vibrating. "What time is it?" she thought aloud. She looked at her phone and realized that it was Deuce texting her, asking her if she was still showing up. Morgan could not believe how calm she felt. Usually she would be anxious and all over the place, but for some odd reason she felt different, as if she had nothing to worry about. She rushed into the bathroom and got herself together to go down to the cafeteria and meet up with Deuce. For the first time, she had no idea what she was going to say or how she was even going to start the conversation out. "Why me," she said to herself looking in the mirror. "Why me…"

As soon as she walked through the corridor of the hospital cafeteria, there was Deuce posted up against the way. "What's up Morgan," stated Deuce. "Everything," exclaimed Morgan. Morgan looked Deuce up and down, but just couldn't bring her mind to believe that her brother was gay and that Deuce was his man. He was fly and everything, she thought to herself…but my brother and him…Seriously!!!! "Morgan….Morgan…," repeated Deuce. "Ohhh, I'm so sorry, my mind is everywhere lately, sorry about that," replied Morgan. "So Deuce, here it is…the streets are tellin' me that my brother is gay, that you're his lover., and that's the reason why his punk ass so called homies did this to him," blurted out Morgan without even thinking. Deuce leaned back in his chair, slowly grazed his butterscotch hands across his beard, and quietly stated, "That's it." "That's why I wanted to talk to you…I knew that he never said anything to you about us, he ain't want nobody to know," explained Deuce. "As far as who did this to him, I'm all ova that, leave your worries for something else," demanded Deuce.

Morgan couldn't stop staring at Deuce, she didn't know what more to say to him. Her mind did not want to believe that Maurice was gay, but her heart and soul told her that it was true. She was mostly in shock at the fact that Maurice never told her anything and that someone would do this to another person in this day and age, in America, all because they were gay. "Look Deuce, none of this is right, especially for it to happen to my brother, someone that bothers no one!" "Much respect for you talking to me, but to be honest with you, I'm just really focused on getting my brother back." "He's doing much better today, maybe you should go up and see him," stated Morgan. Morgan could not believe the words that were coming out of her mouth, they were nothing that she would ever say. "I'm trippin'," she whispered under her breath. "Word...I'll catch you later Morgan," replied Deuce.

As he stood up from his seat to walk about, Morgan raised up as well and headed towards the food station in the cafeteria to grab something to eat. After she sat down with her food, she realized that she hadn't really ate anything in about two days. She was just running so much and so worried about everything with Maurice, that her mind, body, and spirit were all over the place. Right then and there, standing in the hospital cafeteria of all places, Morgan realized that enough was enough and that it was time for her to get herself together. This ride that she has been on in life was not leading her anywhere. She thought to herself, "I could be gone today and what would I leave behind, besides memories of me sliding down some pole and bouncing my behind for a man to think of me only in his secret thoughts." She had no idea what she was going to do, how she was going to do it, but she knew that it was time for her to change her life. It was time and she had wasted enough of hers on absolutely nothing.

Morgan was searching for her phone in her purse so that she could call LaKeya, but couldn't find it for anything. "Shoot, I must have left it up in Maurice's room on the charger," she thought to herself. As she hurried out of the cafeteria and waited for the elevator to come, she continued to search through her purse again and her jacket pocket. When the elevator door opened, she stepped in. After the door of the elevator closed, it opened again and standing there was Chaplin Carrington. "Seriously, not today with this lady," thought Morgan. "Hi there young lady, I hope that all is well with your brother," questioned Chaplin Carrington. Morgan replied, "Thank you for asking, he's doing much better today Ma'am." "Our father will give you all the strength you need while he is healing your loved one, just trust in HIM my child…blessings upon you," stated Chaplin Carrington, as she smiled and exited the elevator. When Morgan reached the fifth floor and turned the corner to her brothers' room, she was happy to be out of the elevator and next to him.

EDQUINA WASHINGTON

Chapter 5
NEW BEGINNINGS AND OLD ENDINGS

It had been a few weeks since Morgan had stepped foot into *Top Shelf*. She knew with every ounce of her that she did not want to go back to dancing, there, or anywhere for that matter. She also knew that she needed to let Fat Kat know face to face that she was done. Although she owed him nothing, all that she could think about was having to deal with his mouth and him being pissed that she was leaving. Fat Kat and Morgan went way back. When she was seventeen years old, he was the only one that would let her dance and make money, without trying to sleep with her, when she left from home. He knew and she knew that he was her last stop before doing whatever she had to do, so that she could eat. Unlike most of the girls that came through Top Shelf, Morgan didn't have their same stories of drug addiction, sexual abuse, raised on the streets, no parents, and all of the other ill wills of society, she was raised in a good home. She lived in a nice house, her parents both had great jobs and nice cars, the only problem was that they both worked about eighty hours a week, which left no time for them to spend with Morgan and Maurice. They were often left alone to their own vices, due to their parents work schedules.

Morgan was always searching for attention, which is why she left home at sixteen years old to be with her then twenty-two year old boyfriend that turned out to be possessive and physically abusive. When she broke away from him, her pride kept her from going back home, and that's when she ran into the opportunity of Top Shelf.

Morgan often thought about her parents and if they loved her or even cared about how she and Maurice's life were. She even wondered if they lived in the same home. Morgan had so much anger, hurt, and resentment in her heart for her parents; for them not spending time with her, not loving her, and not looking for her. She felt as if her leaving and Maurice living his life on the streets hustlin', were an answer to their prayers so that they didn't have to think about taking care of them. Little did she know, she knew nothing of the pain and havoc that she caused in their lives. At the time, Top Shelf appeared to be the silver lining in the cloud, but as time moved on, she realized that it would end up being the constant gray cloud in her life, with no glimmer of hope.

Morgan was in deep thought, until she heard her door bell rang. "Hey Boo, how you feeling?" "You always come at the right time

Keya, it's like you're my angel." Morgan had a true and open conversation with LaKeya about Maurice, him being gay, Deuce being his man, and her realizing that she did not want to dance anymore. She couldn't stop describing to LaKeya the feeling that she experienced when she was around Chaplin Carrington. LaKeya just sat back and listened to Morgan, holding her hands, consoling her and letting her know that she loved her and would always be there for her.

"You should come to church with me on Sunday Morgan." "Keya, you trippin'....me at church...yeah right!" "Alright, you don't know what you're missin'" joked Keya. "I don't and maybe one day I will find out, but today is not that day!" Morgan knew that Keya would throw that lifeline in, as soon as she opened up to her, but she just wasn't ready. Besides, she decided that she needed to be by Maurice's side every day until he fully recovered and that was exactly what she was going to do. LaKeya stayed for a while to keep Morgan company and to make sure that she was doing okay. She could tell that Morgan was going through something, because she normally didn't open up and her house looked a complete mess. Before leaving, LaKeya and Morgan prayed together for her brother's strength to recover and for her to welcome God's presence into her life. Although they have been best friends since middle school, at that moment they both experienced a closeness to each other that was indescribable. Morgan hugged LaKeya tight and promised her that she would give her a call tomorrow.

After the door closed, Morgan just fell to the floor, with her back up against the door in tears. Everything inside of her just felt unleveled. Her thoughts were running rampant through her mind, her heart was racing, and her soul felt uneasy. It was as if, she could physically feel the tug of war that her heart and soul were experiencing and she was standing on the outside of her body watching everything take place.

After calling into the hospital to check in on Maurice, Morgan felt a bit better. She wanted more than anything to relax and get rid of this feeling that she had in the pit of her stomach. Her spirit felt as if it weighed two thousand pounds. Morgan thought to herself if she had always felt this way, but never remained still or silenced long enough to allow this sense of unevenness to envelop her. She settled herself, by remaining in constant thought about everything and anything. She replayed in her mind facing the inevitable disruption of the only piece of life that she has ever known. Every situation of fear comforted her resistance as she sank deeper and deeper into the softness of her cream leather lounge with a glimpse of hope that she could embrace taking a long walk on the path of change in her life. Without notice, her thoughts ceased and she was at rest, lying in the surroundings of silence upon a bed full of worries. No tears, no unsettledness, and nowhere else to run.

Morgan raised up from her lounge and looked at her phone. "Ten-thirty!" She hurried, got dressed and flew out the door. Morgan was determined to handle her business today and hand in her walking papers to Fat Kat. "Damn," she whispered. For some reason her iPod was not working. She wanted more than anything to listen to her girl Sade as she made her way to Top Shelf. That was the only sound that could calm her and put her mind at peace, especially in the traffic she was experiencing on the way. Pulling up to the parking lot of Top Shelf, gave Morgan an uneasy feeling. "Wait…what am I going to say?" she mouthed. "Please give me the strength to end this," she expelled. She looked in her rearview mirror, put on her MAC lip glass, and stepped out the car. Making her way to the door, she heard a few of the regulars calling her name. She hurried in the door and thought to herself, "That's exactly why this is it!"

"What up Mystery, ain't nobody seen you in a minute, damn, I thought you went under or something," joked Lance. "Mind your business Lance, where Fatz at?" "Where he be at!" "You still lookin' good though Mystery," commented Lance. Morgan just walked away, annoyed and aggravated at everything. When she pulled back the crimson curtains to the back and the other ladies noticed her, all conversation and movement came to an abrupt halt. All that you could hear were her size 9 ½ Manolo's hitting the filthy cement floor of Top Shelf heading back to Fatz's office.

"I'm out Fatz," Morgan demanded. "Yeah you been out, who the hell do you think you are walkin' in my spot like you can do whatever the hell you want?" yelled Fat Kat. "Look, I'm out Fatz, this ain't for me no more, my ride is ova here," Morgan explained. "You know you put me in a situation Mystery" "Custy's beggin' for you, nobody can't find you, and I'm left to answer for your shit." "Get your shit and get the fuck outta here Mystery!" "That's how you gonna do me?" "Remember who fed you when you were hungry," yelled Fat Kat. "C'mon Fatz, respect my hustle, I'm respectin' yours enough to let you know my time is done," explained Morgan. "Take it or leave it!" Morgan hissed as she left out of Fat Kat's office. As she walked down the hallway towards her freedom, she kept it moving, parted the curtains, walked past Lance, got in her car, drove out the lot. Halfway down the street, Morgan pulled over. She threw her head back and rested it on her headrest and just gazed at the city street, watching the people walking from corner to corner, cars moving from north to south and just let life sink in. She knew for a fact that today was not the last time that she would have to deal with Fatz, but for some odd reason, she was not worried about it at all. After touching up her make-up, Morgan drove off and headed to the hospital to check in on Maurice. She wanted more than anything to talk to Maurice about how she had been feeling and her leaving Top Shelf, but she didn't want to place her burdens on him and have him carry that weight on his shoulders.

As soon as she reached Maurice's room,

immediately her breathe was taken away by the nauseating smell of cleanliness that the hospital had. She had to train herself to take breaths in slowly until the smell subsided and she no longer recognized it. Morgan bent over to kiss Maurice and just then, his eyes opened. "Maurice, I'm here, don't say anything…I'm here," she expressed with joy. She ran out to the doctor's station and yelled, "he's awake…he's awake." The nurse explained to her that he had been awake and talking all morning and they tried calling her several times, but she didn't answer. "Thank you, thank you so much!" Morgan rushed back to Maurice's side, excited and sitting with a slew of questions in her mind. "What happened Sis?" questioned Maurice. "They didn't tell you anything Reece?" "Nah, I ain't ask these people nothin', c'mon now sis, you know me betta than that!" explained Maurice. "All I remember is bein' on the block out south and bustin' it up with my mans and them." "Yo Reece, you got jumped on some serious shit." Maurice sat half way up in the bed, almost pulling his IV out of his arm. "By who Morgan...who?" "I know you know sis" "I can't wait to get the fuck outta here and get next to whoeva," yelled Maurice.

Morgan could see the anger and frustration all over Maurice's face. "Calm down Reece, not in here, yo!" "This ain't the time or place," stated Morgan. With veins bulging out under his neck, Maurice hissed, "What the fuck is you talkin' bout Sis, something is wrong with you fo' real!" "I'm good Reece, I just don't want you gettin' all upset while you up in here, that's all," expressed Morgan. "Shit, how the hell you think I'm supposed to feel after hearin' some grimmey ass shit like that?" "Knowin' that shit got me in here lookin' like this," explained Maurice. "I know brah...I know!" "We'll deal with that when the time is right, but right now, I need you to get right, so I can stop comin' up in this weird smellin' place," joked Morgan. Maurice fell back into his hospital bed and whispered, "Why me!" "You gonna be aiight Reece, trust me on this!" Morgan didn't know how she knew, but she knew that everything was going to be all right.

Morgan made her way to the nurses' station and to speak with Maurice's doctor. She wanted to know how much longer he had to be here and what if anything she could do to ease his comfort. As Morgan made her way back to Maurice's room, she kept thinking about how she was going to bring up the subject of why he was jumped and her knowing about Deuce. While she never kept much of anything from Maurice, she was still a bit upset that he kept his sexuality a secret from her and that she had to find out this way by someone else. Just as she started to get lost in the show on tv, Maurice's doctor came into the room. "Hi, I'm Dr. Robertson and I've been overseeing your care since your arrival here." "How are you feeling?" questioned Dr. Robertson. "Sore, I can't breathe right and my left arm don't feel right," explained Maurice.

"From the initial damage, I would say that you've had a remarkable recovery," explained Dr. Robertson. "It's nice to see you awake, talking, and responsive." "So, will he be able okay again and how much longer," Morgan questioned Dr. Robertson. "He should regain full recovery, but may have some minor nerve damage to his left arm, we are still in the stages of observation." "1-2 more weeks, depending upon your progress in physical therapy and you should be cleared for release, with weekly physical therapy sessions of course," explained Dr. Robertson. "Good, cuz

I'm ready to be outta here, like today," stated Maurice. "I can understand Sir, but your full recovery is my priority!" "Thank you Dr. Robertson," commented Morgan.

After Dr. Robertson left the room, the conversation between Maurice and Morgan had ceased. All that you could hear was the faint sound of the news anchor on the six o'clock news rambling on. Morgan knew that Maurice's mind was focused on trying to find out who put him in this position and why. She could sense the aggravation that he was feeling, but knew that she could do nothing to keep him from feeling this way, because truth be told, she would be feeling the same exact way if she were in his position. Morgan knew that they had to talk about something and that she wasn't going to spend the next four hours sitting in complete silence next to him, although she knew just how her brother could be.

"I stopped dancing," blurted out Morgan. "Whatever Morgan," exclaimed Maurice as he cut his chestnut eyes at her without even moving his head. "No, I'm serious, I gave Fatz my walkin' papers, I'm done with that life Reece." "I can't take it anymore," expressed Morgan. "That's what's up sis, you didn't need to be doin' that shit anyway, but that was your hustle, so how could I knock you" explained Maurice. "Yeah, I'm just starting to feel different Reece." "It's like I'm thinking about everything and thinking about my future."

"Do you ever think about Mom and Dad?" questioned Morgan. "I wonder if they even know where we are or even care about us." "It's like, we were left to the savages of the world and no one ever came to look for us." "C'mon Sis with all of dat, I don't want to hear that shit," stated Maurice. "Sorry Reece, but it's real and it's what be on my mind constantly." "I just wanted to let you know where I am right now and what's goin' on in my life," stated Morgan. "That's cool sis, ain't tryna make you feel no kinda way, I just don't wanna hear all of that right now," explained Maurice. "I got you brah, I know your love for me ain't stop," expressed Morgan as she smiled and glared at Maurice.

It felt so good to see Maurice up, talking, and moving around. For these past two months, Morgan felt the loneliest that she has ever felt. Not having Maurice there scared her, if she were to be honest, it made her realize that at any moment, her life could be taken away from her and she would have nothing at all to show for it.

Chapter 6
SECRETS BEAR SPOILED FRUITS

Morgan opened her eyes to a complete blur. She looked up at the ceiling and realized that she had fallen asleep in the hospital. As she pulled the blanket from over top of her, she could see the back of Deuce's head, as he was standing next to Maurice's bed. She thought about popping up and trying to see what their reaction would be, but decided to stay lying down, thinking that she would be able to ease drop on their conversation. As much as she tried to, she could only hear their voices, but couldn't make out their words. Morgan closed her eyes and tried to remain still. "What would listening to their conversation prove," she thought. She already knew everything that she needed to know, she just needed to find out if Maurice knew that she was aware of his secret.

Morgan was cold and couldn't take it anymore. She wanted to get up, use the bathroom, talk to Maurice for a bit, go home and get up out of the cold ass hospital. Morgan slowly got up from the chair, threw the blanket to the side, grabbed her purse and went into the bathroom. She didn't say anything to Maurice or Deuce. Morgan wanted Maurice to know that she was up, but didn't want to say anything to Deuce, to keep the air calm between her and Maurice. Morgan started to brush her teeth in the bathroom, when she heard the door close to Maurice's room. She washed her face and looked into the mirror. She looked at every inch of her face, her even chocolate skin tone, the shape of her almond eyes, her small petite nose, and the fullness of her lips. "So this is what I look like…not bad," she whispered to herself.

Morgan was so used to passing through life in a complete rush that she rarely paid attention to what was truly beneath her makeup. She took her hands, rubbed her face in a downward motion, grabbed her lotion out of the bag and rubbed it on her face and hands. Morgan became anxious. She knew that her thoughts of leaving the hospital in a hurry were over and that she and Maurice were about to get down and dirty with their conversation about him being gay. "Sis, what you doin' in there?" yelled Maurice. Morgan opened the door staring Maurice straight in the eyes. "So now you wanna talk!" "Sis look, c'mon this is hard as hell to explain," expressed Maurice. "I just didn't know how to tell you, Morgan." Morgan walked close to Maurice, hovered over top of him, and whispered "How do you think I feel when everyone else knows what's goin' down, except your own flesh and blood?" "What part of the game is that?" "Keepin' secrets and shit," hissed Morgan as she turned around and walked towards the window. "I tell you everything Reece…everything." She could feel her ears getting hot and her heart racing as she thought more and more about Maurice keeping his sexuality a secret from her. "Sis, just listen to me, yo…sit down and listen to me," pleaded Maurice. Morgan didn't budge; she continued to remain standing, facing the window, refusing to look at Maurice in the face. She was hurt that he would keep something from her and immediately began to think what else he was keeping from her that she didn't know. Maurice begin to explain that he had always felt different and that he knew he was attracted to men, but often times tried to put those thoughts in the back of his mind, because of what his boys and everyone else would think.

He explained that although he had slept with and dated several girls, he was never really into them and that's why he ran through them like it wasn't nothin'. Maurice shared that Deuce was a connect down in VA, they got close and one thing led to another. By this time, Morgan had turned around facing Maurice, completely speechless. "So how did your boyz know?" "Did you tell any of them?" "Did your boo Deuce tell any of them?" "Look Sis, I don't know…I really don't know!" "And cut it with the boo comments yo," demanded Maurice. "Somebody had to say something, unless y'all was all kissed up and holdin' hands, while on the block," stated Morgan rudely. "Fuck you Morgan, this is my life," snickered Maurice. "Yeah and we see where YOUR life got you and we see who's by your side," yelled Morgan. "I can't believe you

Reece, I really can't! "The strangest shit is happenin' and it's all on my time," shared Morgan. "I can't do this right now, it's too freakin' early, I need to take a shower and get myself situated," explained Morgan.

As Morgan grabbed her belongings in anger and turned to walk towards the door, she looked back at Maurice, shook her head and kept it moving. There was so much more that she wanted to scream on Maurice about, but she knew that he needed to heal, but the day, hour, and minute that he left that hospital, she promised herself that it was on!

Once she got through the door, she searched for her phone and called LaKeya. There was so much that she had to tell her. It was abnormal for her not to speak to LaKeya at least once or more during the week, but with all of the drama that was going on in her life, it was starting to get in the way of her relationship with her best friend. LaKeya and Morgan were on the phone for almost two hours, but it felt like fifteen minutes. They talked about everything, including Maurice and Deuce and Maurice improving in the hospital.

"So, what's up with you Morgan?" questioned LaKeya. "Just tryna maintain." "Everything seems to be moving by so fast, but I still feel like I'm standing still," answered Morgan. "Hey that's life, everything can't work out for us all the time," commented LaKeya. "So how's my baby girl doing…and how's Damian?" questioned Morgan. "Joy is doing good girl, there is always something new with her, she is a mess." "Girl…and Damian…is Damian, what can I say," explained LaKeya. "When our elders told us that marriage is hard work, girl….they were not lying!" "Some days I think to myself, what was I thinking, then I look at Joy and I get the answer to my question," explained LaKeya. "See that's why you're the one married with children and I am not," joked Morgan.

"So, how did things go with leavin' Top Shelf?" questioned LaKeya. "Straight chaos, but I got out." "Fatz is mad, but he'll get over it, I don't understand why he acts like there ain't a revolving door of dancers coming through there," explained Morgan. "You don't know how happy I am that you're outta there boo," expressed LaKeya. "You should come to church with us tomorrow Morgan, Joy would be so excited to see you there!" expressed LaKeya. "Owwww...you know you're wrong, throwin' Joy's name up in there, that's dirty Keya….real dirty," joked Morgan. "I'll let you know Keya, give Joy a kiss for me, I gotta go." "Cool and Morgan...stop being mad at Maurice, forgive your brother and let it go," commented LaKeya. With that, Morgan hung up the phone and smiled. Lakeya always had to have the last word, no matter what. Morgan especially hated when she knew Lakeya was right and this was one of those moments.

Although Morgan felt much better that she and LaKeya got the chance to talk, she knew that there was more that LaKeya wanted to talk about and so did she! Talking with LaKeya always gave her a new prospective on life and that's why she loved her. There was nothing like having someone by her side that would always be there for her, no matter what and someone that would let her know when she needed to get it together, even if, she didn't want to hear it. Morgan knew deep down inside, that it was the prayers of LaKeya that kept her from ending up in worse situations and traveling down the long lost road that she had seen many others travel down and never return.

After the long day that she had, Morgan made up her mind that she was going to spend some time relaxing and pampering herself. It had been about a month since she got a fill in, pedicure, and massage. Although she was allowing the unpredictability of change to creep into her life, there was one thing that would remain constant and that would be her ultimate understanding for the need to treat yourself to the good things in life. Morgan couldn't get through the door of Salon Beaute' before her nail tech blew her spot up and started to joke with her about them not seeing her in a long time. Morgan was smart about keeping the places that she would frequent far from her life as a dancer. Salon Beaute' was miles from her natural habitat, which provided her with a sense of escape.

Nothing or no one that walked through those doors, were at all, remnants of the life that she had led, once she exited and stood on the outside of their doors. They treated her like a Queen and never questioned her about her life, which was the main reason she chose that location as her comfort zone.

Morgan felt phenomenal once she made it back home from Salon Beaute'. She decided to stay in, take a long hot bath and get some rest. Toe first, she dipped her foot into the steaming hot bath. The warmth of the water and the evaporation of the steam immediately left Morgan with a feeling of tranquility. She closed her eyes and allowed her mind to run empty with thoughts. Morgan felt good and that is all that she allowed her mind to think about. She went to bed that night, in a peaceful spirit for the first time in a long time. Morgan made up her mind that she would attend church with LaKeya and her family. She thought, "what could it hurt."

Chapter 7
CAN WE SAY "CHUUUUUUUUUUURCH?"

It was 9:45 and Morgan woke up well rested. She texted LaKeya that she would be going to church and that she would meet them there. Morgan stayed lying in bed, trying to piece outfits together in her head to wear to church. "What am I going to wear," she thought to herself. She got up from her bed and stood in front of her closet, pulling out dress after dress to wear, but none of them were acceptable for church. "This don't make no sense," she whispered to herself. After spending fifteen minutes feverishly going through her wardrobe, she finally found a gold dress that she had forgotten about to wear. Morgan was always late for everything, but today, she made a vow to herself that she would be on time.

She pulled into the parking lot of *Glory Mountain Baptist Church* feeling uncertain about the unknown. The last time that Morgan had been inside of a church was for Joy's christening ceremony and before that, it had been her eighth-grade year in the Salvation Army summer camp. Morgan watched as all the seasoned women walked into church in their finely sculptured colorful suits with grand hats to match. "Go ahead sista," she commented to herself in the car. Morgan felt like she was watching a fashion show entitled "Sunday's Best." You could sense in their walk that they were proud and knew that they were as sharp as a tack.

Morgan texted LaKeya to let her know that she was here. LaKeya texted back, "I'm in the lobby waiting for you." Morgan grabbed her ounce of courage and walked towards the doors of *Glory Mountain Baptist Church*. As she got closer, she could hear the hymns being sung. As promised, there was LaKeya, looking as radiant as ever. "Hey boo, c'mon we have a seat for you," whispered LaKeya. Morgan tried her best not to stare at people as she made her way to her seat, but she couldn't help to notice how full the church was. She sat down softly on the bench style seating and without notice; Joy jumped into her lap and gave her a kiss and big hug. Joy was most definitely given the proper name, because that is all she brought whenever she was around. Joy pleaded with her mother to sit next to her and Auntie Morgan during service and without a doubt, she got what she wanted. Morgan watched as various members of the church arose from their seats and began to worship during the service, whether they just silently stood, yelled comments, or stood and raised their hands in agreement. The choir got up and began to sing "How Great Is Our God." Morgan listened, as she allowed the lead soprano songbird minister to her spirit. The Pastor's sermon was okay, Morgan thought to herself. He touched on some points, but nothing that made her give consideration to handing over her life to Christ. She still did not understand the entire concept and wasn't at the point in her life that she was willing to have that conversation with anyone.

Morgan was exiting the church, when she noticed a few of her customers from Top Shelf. "Imagine that," she chuckled to herself. Aaliyah's famed hit song, "If your girl only knew" ran through her mind. Morgan couldn't wait to bust it up with LaKeya later on about this. It wasn't that she couldn't believe it, it was the mere fact that it was happening right in front of her face, as if she was watching a prime time movie about her life. She then thought, "I wonder if they noticed me." LaKeya hugged Morgan and thanked her for finally taking her up on her invitation to attend church. "How did you like it?" questioned LaKeya. "It was different and interesting at the same time, but we gotta talk boo," exclaimed Morgan. "Ohhh no...I don't even want to know," joked LaKeya. "Yeah you do, you know you do, I'll call you later" stated Morgan. Morgan gave Damian and Joy a hug and made her way to the parking lot. "So this is what church is all about." "How does Keya sit up in there every Sunday?" Morgan thought to herself. Morgan turned her car on and reached for her purse to check her phone. She noticed that she had a missed call from Sugar. "I wonder what she wants," Morgan thought.

Morgan called Sugar back, which was a

conversation that would take her from church to the hospital thirty minutes later. "Yo Mystery, it ain't the same without you around," stated Sugar. "I know it's not, but I ain't comin' back Sugar." "I'm sorry," explained Morgan. "So what you doin' that you're not comin' back?" "Why did you just bounce like that," Sugar questioned. "It was just my time baby girl, that's all I can tell you," Morgan commented. "You will know when your time is!" "Remember what I told you, don't let Top Shelf break your spirit Sugar, use it as a step up to something else, don't get stuck like I did," expressed Morgan. "I hear you Mystery, but without you here, it just don't feel right," Sugar explained. "Hey, what can I say," joked Morgan. "Call me if you need me Boo, you know I got your back," expressed Morgan. "Cool, I'll holla," answered Sugar. Morgan really liked Sugar and knew that she could do way better than becoming a slave to the confines of

Top Shelf, but it was her only resort to surviving this life. She knew firsthand how it felt to be young, hungry, homeless and needing something quick and fast to get on your feet that turns into your everyday life, before you realize that you have sacrificed your innocence for the sinful pleasures of others.

Morgan was walking from the hospital garage, when she seen Ty leaving out the hospital doors. She tried to increase the gait of her walk to get to him, but he had disappeared in the darkness of the garage and she knew that was the wrong place to roll up on him. "Why was he here!" She pushed open Maurice's hospital door to find him gone. "Where's my brother," she yelled as she ran towards the nurses' station. "He just went down for x-ray, he should be back shortly," answered the nurse. Morgan felt an extreme sign of relief. She had thought that Ty had come and finished her brother off in the hospital. Morgan waited patiently for Maurice to return to the room.

While awaiting his return, as usual she began to freshen up his room and make it feel as comfortable as possible. After the nurse brought him back in and walked out the door, Morgan blurted out, "Ty was here to see you?" "Damn sis, you the FBI now?" "You ain't neva got on my nerves this much, you need to go back to dancin' or find something to do with your time," commented Maurice. "You are my time Reece, so what's good?" questioned Morgan. "Nothin' that you need to worry about, I got this sis, it's my battle and I'll fight it," demanded Maurice. "Whatever battle you gotta fight, I'm here to fight it with you!" "I thought this was understood years ago, so I don't know why you speakin' to me like I'm somebody new!" hissed

Morgan angrily! "I'm here, even if you don't want me here and that's that!" exclaimed Morgan. "Straight like that…huh sis?" Maurice joked with Morgan. She smiled and just shook her head.

Maurice knew that he was nothing without Morgan by his side and Morgan knew the same. They always fought and made up quickly, Maurice knew that Morgan was a fighter since they were younger, because she would never give up on any situation. She was always willing to face problems head on. Morgan shared with Maurice her experience from church and how she seen a few customers from Top Shelf there. She and Maurice just chuckled. Morgan explained to Maurice that she always hears of people explaining how they just get a feeling when they go to church and just give their lives over to Christ and that she didn't feel anything like that when she went to church with LaKeya and her family. "Sis, you ain't like everybody else," commented Maurice. "If that's what you looking for, then it'll find you," explained Maurice. "I ain't lookin' for that, I was just sayin'," explained Morgan.

Morgan went to the hospital cafeteria to get something to eat. She decided to get Maurice something as well. He was complaining the entire time she was there today about how disgusting his hospital food was. While waiting in line to pay for her food, she felt a soft tap on her left shoulder. Morgan turned to find Chaplin Carrington standing behind her smiling. "How are you today my child?" questioned Chaplin Carrington. "I'm doing well, how are you," commented Morgan. "By the grace of God, I'm making it around," commented Chaplain Carrington. "How is your brother doing sweetheart?" questioned Chaplain Carrington.

"Oh, he is doing so much better, he should be leaving the hospital by the end of next week," Morgan explained gleefully. "May God Bless you both," expressed Chaplain Carrington. "Thank you so much Chaplin Carrington," commented Morgan. As soon as Morgan gave the clerk her money and turned to see where Chaplin Carrington had went, she was gone. "That lady is always saying something," she thought to herself.

Morgan laughed at the expression on Maurice's face when she got back to the room and laid out the chicken cheesesteak and fries that she brought from the cafeteria. "Thanks sis," he commented with a huge smile on his face. "Look at you…salivating over there like a lion about to damage his prey," joked Morgan. "Yeah, that's exactly what it's gonna be right about now," Maurice commented. Morgan stayed with Maurice at the hospital for a few more hours, then eventually made her way home. She had a full day and had thoughts galore sprinting through her mind. Morgan knew that she had a lot of thinking and planning to do, but had no idea what she was planning or how she was going to do whatever she was planning. She started to feel like her entire life had instantly been peaked on this mountain of change; the only problem was that it did not come with any directions for the path ahead in which she was traveling.

As soon as Morgan got home, she knew that the most important thing that she had to do was portion out her stash to determine how much longer she could survive without having any income coming in. After counting everything, she only had $22,000, which would last her about eight to ten months, if she didn't have any out of the ordinary expenses. "What am I going to do," she thought. Spending her entire time focused and saturated in one area left little room for any type of exploration. Morgan had never taken the time to think about goals for herself, other than how much money she was going to make in a week. She hadn't had a drink of alcohol in over one month and felt that she deserved to have one of her favorite drinks. She fixed herself a Rum and coke and started cooking dinner. Three drinks and a full stomach later, she allowed her couch to become her resting place. Morgan slept peacefully that night. She didn't care if her calmness was induced and allowed for a temporary release of her issues, in her mind, it was all well worth not having to face them for a day.

Wednesday morning greeted Morgan with a throbbing headache and sore joints. With her clothes still on from the night before, she awoke lying on her couch, thinking, "what the hell happened?" Immediately, she got up and with dizziness, fell right back down. She sat still for a few minutes in deep thought about the time and the last place she remembered leaving her cell phone. Once she realized that she left it in the kitchen when she was cooking, she eased off the couch and made her way over to her island to find that it was 10:47am and that she had seven missed calls from LaKeya, and a text message that read, "we need to talk, let's do lunch today?" Morgan just looked at her phone. She was not in any condition to talk with LaKeya and knew that LaKeya could tell that she was drinking. For some odd reason, she felt kind of guilty about her drinking and didn't want LaKeya to find out. She wondered what was so urgent that she had to talk, but knew that she would be there. She texted LaKeya back, "yup, let's do Finley's at 12:15."

Morgan called to check on her brother before she went to the hospital. "You aiight Reece?" "I'm good, trying to maintain." "Cool, I'll be there after I do lunch with Keya," explained Morgan. "Aiight, see you then sis."

When Morgan walked into the restaurant, she began looking around for LaKeya. As soon as she turned to her left, she noticed her sitting in the third row near the window, not looking like herself. Morgan quickly went into defense mode. "Who do we need to roll up on Keya?" questioned Morgan. "You know I always come prepared for any situation." "I don't like the look on your face or the person who put it there right about now," stated LaKeya. "Calm down Morgan, you are a mess," stated LaKeya. "I'm okay, just a lot of things going on and I need to talk to my bestie," explained LaKeya. "Well look, let's order and then we can talk, because

I'm starvin'," stated Morgan.

Once their food was ordered, LaKeya opened up about an affair that she had been having with a co-worker that was beginning to flourish into more than just an affair. Morgan sat there, with her mouth literally hanging open. For the life of her, she could not believe this conversation was coming out of LaKeya's mouth. With tears forming in her eyes, LaKeya eloquently rationalized her deceit. "It all started with a simple lunch meeting, filled with consistent flirting and then before I knew it, it was me and him sneaking around here and there filling our selfish needs." "I feel so bad Morgan, but at the same time, he is giving me all of the things that Damian is not," confessed LaKeya.

"Damian is an excellent father and husband, but after all these years, I feel like I'm losing the love that I once felt for him." "It just isn't fun like it used to be, and I want that fun," exclaimed LaKeya. Morgan was speechless for a moment. As hungry as she was, she had only taken two bites out of her food, which was now cold. She wanted to jump across the table and slap some sense into her best friend. The picture perfect family that Morgan once thought existed between LaKeya and Damian was now gone. She knew that they had to have rough times and a few challenges, but never anything as scandalous as this. Full of questions, Morgan let them rip. "Do you think Damian knows?" "Who is this guy?" "Is he married too?" "What are you going to do?" "What about Joy?" "I know, boo, no Damian does not know, at least I don't think so…..his name isn't important….he isn't married…..I have no idea what I am going to do, and Joy is fine.

"Every day I wake up saying that today is

the day that I tell him it's over and then I see him, he says something so sweet, or has roses waiting for me on my desk, or walks near me and I just can't end it." "I don't want to break up my family, how would Joy feel?" "I'm not strong enough to walk away from this right now," explained LaKeya. "Keya what is wrong with you boo, you have a good man, a beautiful little girl, a home, and a calm life….do you know what someone like me would do for that?" questioned Morgan. "You know I ain't never been married before, but I do know that this is not you," explained Morgan. "What is going on Keya, I'm the one giving advice and you are the one with the issue, we gotta turn this table around." "Look, you know I'm here for you no matter what boo, but you gotta fix this and figure out what you're going to do," exclaimed Morgan. As they got up to leave the restaurant, Morgan hugged LaKeya tightly and whispered in her ear,

"I love you boo, it's gonna be aiight."

Morgan drove away from Finley's in a trance. She could not believe that LaKeya was going through this. She was just with them in church and everything seemed to be good between them. LaKeya was always the stable and secure one with the sound mind. LaKeya's situation surely proved to her that at that moment, anything could happen and no one is exempt from losing themselves in the grey areas of life.

EDQUINA WASHINGTON

Chapter 8
OPPORTUNITIES KNOCK

"I'm not dancin' anymore and I need somethin' to do," whispered Morgan to herself as she was looking in the mirror at the gym. Although she was positive that the days in the life of Mystery were gone, she still wanted to keep her exquisite physique. She could begin to see changes in her body, from not working out anymore to keep up with her old profession, so she decided to start going to the gym again. "That workout killed me," Morgan joked to the lady next to her. "I don't know if I'm gonna be able to take this Zumba class again, my goodness," she carried on. She showered and made her way out of the gym. As she was walking to the parking lot to get into her car, she seen Lace and some dude in a car arguing. Morgan just shook her head. She thought about the day she fought Lace in *Top Shelf* and felt bad about it. Morgan continued to look into the car as she got closer and she could see how much Lace had changed and that she didn't look much like she used to. She knew that look all too well. The weight of Top Shelf had balanced itself over Lace's life, leaving her in the lost sea of addiction and bad relationships just to keep her life moving. She thought to herself "That was almost me."

Morgan was grateful for the transitions that she had made. In the last three months, she had been attending church for service about twice a month and Bible Study every week. She realized that she enjoyed Bible Study more than Sunday church service. The method of the Bible Study instructor and the simple way that she explained the Bible and faith made sense to Morgan, in a way that she could comprehend and relate the experiences in the Bible to situations in her own life. She realized that she truly enjoyed learning and growing from the word of God. Morgan could see her entire outlook on life changing before her very eyes. She was beginning to take better care of herself, focused on creating goals, and began dealing with some of the guilt she was carrying for past hurt that she had caused others.

Morgan wished that she could share the goodness of her feelings with Maurice. She would often try, when she would check in on him, since he was released from the hospital. She could tell that he was depressed. Maurice was now bound to a wheelchair and needed help from others to survive. Morgan was beginning to spend most of her days at Maurice's house, helping him with his necessities, cooking his food, cleaning, and doing all of the things that he needed. If it were not for Morgan, Maurice would have been left alone.

She would always try her best to remain positive and would share a bit about her experiences in Bible Study. Maurice would listen, but she knew that he was only doing just that, listening, because she was there to help. She would often pray for Maurice when in church or at Bible Study. She honestly didn't know what else she could do. Morgan had decided that maybe she would be interested in becoming a Social Worker or Case Worker and considered registering for college, but had no idea how to even begin the process.

Soon after he was home from the hospital, Deuce stopped coming around and began playing a smaller and smaller role in Maurice's life.

Morgan wanted so much for her old Reece to come back, but she knew that it would be a while or maybe even never.

"Hey Reece, what's good today?" "Seriously sis?" "Just tryna have a conversation with my brother that's all," expressed Morgan. She made her way over to the kitchen to begin making lunch for them. "So what you wanna eat?" "Whatever," hissed Maurice. Morgan was in a hurry to get Maurice's food ready, because for once, she had plans today. She wanted to get online and search for colleges. Morgan was excited about venturing into these new avenues. She wanted to share them with Maurice, but knew that he would steal her joy, so she gave him his lunch, curled up on the chair next to him and focused her entire attention on the screen of her laptop. She couldn't believe how expensive one year of college was, and to think, she would need to attend for an entire four years. Morgan didn't want to, but she knew she would have to get a job, if she were ever going to be able to afford to go to school, she just had no idea where to work. She thought about working somewhere that she could dress up, that wouldn't require her to do too much work, something like a front desk job. Morgan made it a goal that for that week, that she would try to look for some front desk jobs.

She looked over at Maurice to see that he was watching TV. Morgan hated the silence that existed between the both of them. The look on his face told his entire story of frustration and sadness. He was ousted by his friends, he couldn't hustle anymore, and now he was left out to hang dry by his boyfriend. Morgan knew that Maurice felt that he had nowhere to go and no one to confide in. Although she knew that he knew she cared, she knew that it wasn't the same as havin' his boys by his side and being able to get up and do him.

"Reece you ever thought about just leavin' here and buildin' a new life somewhere?," questioned Morgan. "Never thought about it.....where you talkin' bout?" questioned Maurice. "Nowhere in particular, I've just been thinking about it," answered Morgan. "Sis you crazy, always thinking about stuff and ready to just jump ship and keep it movin'" "That's one of the things that I've always loved about you, you don't let things bother you too long, before you just move on," expressed Maurice.

Maurice remembered how head strong Morgan was, even throughout their childhood. Morgan making the decision to leave home in their senior year and just do her, dabbling in hustlin', her career at Top Shelf, and her recent decision to drastically change herself, were all true indicators that she was a strong-minded woman. She was always able to make quick decisions on her feet and never hide behind their consequences or achievements. Even though she was still the same, he could sense that Morgan was becoming a new person and he liked it.

"Reece, I'm about to be out, I got things to do at my own house," commented Morgan. "Cool sis, thanks, I'll holla at you later," "You need to hook me up with one of those little church friends of yours," joked Maurice. "What, I thought you were gay….gotta go Reece" "You need to get yo' life together," exclaimed Morgan, as she cut her eyes at Maurice, grabbed her purse and keys, and made her way out of the door. Morgan knew that Maurice was at a crossroad and she just hoped that he would find his place again.

As usual, Bible study had begun, just as Morgan creeped in and sat in the third to the last pew. She tried hard to make it on time, but it never failed that she was late. Not too many of the women in bible study were friendly to Morgan. They often glanced at her or cut their eyes and gave her a quick hi or wave of the hand, as they looked her up and down. Although she wanted to appear that she wasn't too worried about it, she was becoming a bit discouraged. She started to feel like an outcast.

Morgan knew that some of them knew that she used to be a stripper, just by the looks that they gave her. She knew that she was new to the church and assumed that she would have been welcomed, but she was not. Although she wasn't trying to fit it, she just thought that there would be a bit more hospitality in the house of the Lord. She thought to herself, "If I can fight back my feelings to beat all of their asses, I'm sure they can say Hi and mean it!"

Morgan caught herself staring into space, not paying much attention to the Associate Pastor leading bible study, when she felt a tap on her left shoulder and the voice of a gentleman saying, "Excuse me." Annoyingly, Morgan looked up and met the chestnut brown eyes of a clean shaven gentleman adorned in a caramel complexion, with pulled back unkept dredlocks. "Ummmm," Morgan thought to herself. "Sure," she whispered under her breathe and slid down the church pew, just enough to give him room to be close enough to her. "He looks good, but he's probably gay," Morgan thought to herself. It had been a while since she was attracted to a man and wondered why she was becoming attracted to one right now and of all places….in church. Morgan had to regain focus and remember that she was in church, but was very glad about the company that chose to share the pew with her that day.

Bible study was over and just like clockwork, as she began to gather her things and walk down the opposite side of the pew towards the aisle, he spoke to her. "Hi, I'm Allen." "I'm Morgan, how are you?" "You're new to the church right?" "Yeah…and," questioned Morgan. "Just trying to be friendly, that's all, nothing more," commented Allen defensively. "Cool, see you around," commented Morgan as she grabbed the rest of her stuff and finished her walk down the aisle and out the door. "Seriously, he tried to holla at me in church," she thought to herself. Morgan could not believe that this had happened to her. She didn't want to be naive about the situation, but just could not believe that a guy actually tried to pick her up in church.

As soon as she got in the car, she couldn't wait to call LaKeya and tell her about what happened. "Hey Boo, what's good?" questioned Morgan. "I'm not doing much, what's good with you?" "You seem happy about something," stated LaKeya. "Gurlllllllllllll, I called to tell you about this brotha that tried to holla at me at bible study." "My goodness, even the church men are out front with their prowling," commented Morgan. "Be careful Morgan, the ones in church are the slickest," LaKeya joked, but serious at the same time. "What….they ain't never gonna pull one over on me, but he did look good though…and he smelt soooooooo damn good," Morgan confessed. "Look at you all excited, what was bible study about tonight?" LaKeya questioned. "Girl, I don't even know, I was rudely interrupted by some caramel goodness. They both started laughing. "Morgan, you crazy, I ain't foolin' up with your crazy behind," joked

LaKeya. "Thank you for that laugh girl, I needed that," LaKeya expressed. "Today has been a rough day, Damian and I were arguing earlier." "I think that he knows something is going on." "He wants to go to counseling and I do, but I'm just so caught up," confessed LaKeya. "I'm afraid to let go and afraid that Damian will find out and let me go," LaKeya explained. "Damn Keya, you put the truth in being between a rock and a hard place," Morgan commented. "It'll be all good boo, in due time." "I love you boo, I can tell that you're frustrated," expressed Morgan. "Aiight Morgan, I'm gonna get off this phone and get Joy ready for bed." "You get your hot and fired up self to bed...Miss pick up men in church," joked LaKeya. "Hayyyyyyyyy," exclained Morgan before she hung up the phone.

Morgan was giving some thought to it and realized that she hadn't dated or been with a man sexually in over nine months. The thoughts of Allen were sending her feelings into overdrive. She knew that she would run into him again and was excited thinking about all of the things she would say to flirt with him. Morgan had never been in a relationship, other than her high school boyfriend that she left home for and quickly found herself in an abusive relationship. Once she dated men and they found out that she was a stripper, most never stuck around too long. The constant questioning if she was cheating, how many men tried to talk to her, and demands for her to leave her lifestyle as a stripper, were all common denominators when it came to the reasoning behind her being without a man. At the time, it just wasn't a priority for her, but now, Morgan believed that she had the time and was on the right path to begin dating again.

She pulled out her notes from her internet

search earlier and begin to look over them. "This decision is too hard," she thought to herself. "I got to get with Keya to help me with this!" Morgan felt that she was in a good place, but was also coming to the point where she needed to have some steady money coming in. She had no idea what she could do. The only thing that she knew how to do was dancing.

She combed through the newspaper to see if there was anything that stuck out to her. Things were becoming discouraging. Morgan was beginning to feel as if she had made the wrong decision. She thought about looking to see where else she could dance for a bit to earn a little more money. She just couldn't stomach the embarrassment of going back to Top Shelf, besides Fat Kat would never take her back after their last interaction. Deep down, Morgan really didn't want to do this, but she felt as if she had no choice. Her bills needed paid and her money was running low. Morgan poured herself a double shot of Courvoisier, fell across her bed and allowed the numbness that she grew so used to feeling to massage her emotions and temporarily erase them, for the meantime. Doing things the right way was becoming a narrowed tunnel and Morgan felt stuck at the end. She could see something through the narrow view, but wasn't sure what it was, and was becoming bent out of shape trying to figure it all out. She finally started to realize just how Maurice was feeling and understood that she could not blame him, because she too was beginning to feel the same way.

The more she thought, the more the softness of her down comforter and pillows placed her on a cloud. She was at a place where she could separate from her issues of today and meet the uncertainty of tomorrow. Although it wasn't the best way to experience peace, for now, it was the choice way.

EDQUINA WASHINGTON

Chapter 9
NOTHING IS CONSTANT BUT CHANGE

Bible study was becoming comfortable to Morgan. She was learning, she was growing, and she could sense that she was developing a personal relationship with God. She felt safe for once in her life. Safe enough to ask questions and be open about going through a transition, although Morgan was smart enough not to be too open and specific in a room full of strangers. Morgan shared with the members of her bible study some of the struggle that she had been having with finding a job and not knowing what she was really good at. After bible study was over, Morgan could sense that Allen wanted to talk with her, by the way he kept his eyes and his smile focused on her. "See you later," Morgan whispered as she waved goodbye to Allen. "Morgan, hold up for a minute," Allen boasted. "I knew it," Morgan thought to herself. She waited by the last pew as Allen boldly made his way to her side. "Let's talk outside, I wanna ask you something," commented Allen. "It would be an honor, if you would say yes to dinner with me Friday or Saturday night," expressed Allen. "I can do that," Morgan blurted out. "That would be nice." "So, how can I get in touch with you to finalize our plans?" Allen questioned. "What's your number, I'll call you and you'll have mine," Morgan flirtingly answered yes and exchanged numbers. "Got it, we'll talk later." "Aiight," Morgan answered.

She walked to her car and couldn't wait to get in and scream!!! With a huge smile lit across her face, she let out a huge sign of excitement.

All she could think about was the curve in Allen's lips when he was talking to her and the relaxed way his locs sat on his shoulders. "I gotta call Keya," she commented loudly. Just then, her phone buzzed and of course, it was Allen messaging her to tell her to have a good night. Morgan just smirked and thought to herself, "classic move." Allen was most definitely easy on the eyes and a man about God, but at the end of the day, he was still a man; and in her mind subject to more than meets the eyes. He appeared to be someone that could help keep her in the right direction, but then again, she could be wrong. After feeling depressed for the past couple of weeks, she was elated to have something in her life that excited her and moved her focus from worry. She had been so caught up in worrying about her situation and Maurice that it left little time for her to think about being happy herself.

On her way to Maurice's house, Morgan called LaKeya and spilled the beans about her upcoming date and how good it felt to have someone actually take the time to be interested in her, without knowing her past. LaKeya seemed generally excited about Morgan's newfound happiness and appeared to be in a great mood. "So when are y'all going to go out to eat and where?" questioned LaKeya. "I'm thinking Saturday and he can take me to Finley's," "I'll feel more comfortable in our spot," explained Morgan. "Girl, you done got yourself a date," joked LaKeya. "Morgan, it's about time," expressed LaKeya. "Have fun and keep an open mind," LaKeya expressed. "I know you ain't tellin' me what to do, Miss slidin' on her husband," stated Morgan. "Owwww, you got me, whatever...." "I still love you though boo, but you did me dirty right there," explained LaKeya. "I'm just sayin....that's all!" The laughter between both of them erupted at the same time as usual.

LaKeya loved Morgan's straightforward approach and Morgan loved LaKeya's compassionate ways, something that she never had, even as a child. Morgan could feel that she and LaKeya began getting a bit closer since she had started attending church and LaKeya started opening up about the issues in her marriage.

Morgan almost forgot that she had to stop by the pharmacy to pick up Maurice's meds. If she would've thought about it ten seconds later, she would've missed her turn and would have to drive another five blocks before she could turn around. As she walked through the door, to her surprise, there right in front of her was Chaplin Carrington on her way out. "Hi Chaplin Carrington." "Well hi there, young lady," answered Chaplin Carrington. "How are you and how is the health of your family member?" questioned Chaplin Carrington. "I'm doing okay, just looking for work and my brother is healing well, thanks for asking," explained Morgan. "Something will come your way, I know they're hiring at the two nursing homes on the east end of town near the shopping center; as good as you cared for your family member in the hospital, I'm sure you would be great working there," Chaplin Carrington shared. "Thank you, I'm gonna check that out," Morgan replied. As Chaplin Carrington reached in to give Morgan a hug, she softly stated, "Bless you my child." Seeing Chaplin Carrington surely lifted her spirits as well. Morgan always felt calmed by her. She was glad that she ran into her and that she gave her the information on the nursing homes hiring, but just wasn't sure that it was something that she could do.

She walked into Maurice's apartment to find him still in bed sleeping, with remnants of a blunt lying next to him on his nightstand. Morgan just shook her head. She couldn't really say much about Maurice evaporating in the branches of weed, when she was doing the same with alcohol. His apartment looked a mess. Dishes and empty takeout boxes were piled up on the kitchen table, sink, and counters. Morgan was disgusted at the look of Maurice's place. It had only been three days since she was last here and it looked like it had been more like three weeks. Although she felt sorry for Maurice, she knew that it was time for him to start taking some responsibility for himself, but just didn't know how to break it to him without it starting an argument.

While finishing up cleaning, Morgan could hear Maurice getting up. "It's me Reece, just cleanin' up your nasty ass place." "I need to take my key back, you just roll up in here like this is your place." "Excuse me....you don't appreciate anything, I could have spent my last two hours doing something for me, but no............I'm here trying to help my sorry ass brother out," pleaded Morgan. "I ain't ask you to come here," Maurice shamelessly blurted out. "What....look because I'm your sister and ain't nobody else gonna come here and put up with your mouth, I'm gonna make you somethin' to eat as fast as I can and make moves," Morgan expressed.

Moving across the room in his wheel chair, Maurice sucked his teeth and turned the TV on. Morgan was pissed. She could not believe that Maurice shot his mouth off at her like that. She could tell that he was really depressed and she didn't know what to do to bring him out of it and realized that it was not the right moment to talk.

Morgan stayed to cook his food, because she knew that he had no one other than her coming over to talk with him. She knew that Maurice becoming a recluse was not doing either of them any good. She made up her mind that night that she was going to do something that would piss her off, if he ever did it to her. She was going to call Deuce, find out why he left her brother and see if he had any advice on what to do to help him.

"Reece, here's your food, the extra is in the fridge and I brought you more juice and milk," explained Morgan. "I love you brah, call me if you need me," expressed Morgan. After she walked out the door and down the hall, she broke down in tears. It was just too much to bear seeing Maurice in the condition that he was. She wanted more than anything to just jump on him and hug him, tell him that everything will be alright, and then make it alright, but she knew that wasn't reality. "Why god…why," she silently whispered. Just then, she heard some kids coming up the steps of the building and quickly wiped the tears from her face. They were giggling and having a good time, what Morgan wouldn't give to experience that joy.

As soon as she hit her front door, her phone rang. "Hey Allen." "Hey Morgan, how was your day?" "Long…how was yours?" "I had a blessed day," replied Allen. "Good for you," Morgan thought to herself. She really didn't feel like talking to Allen and didn't even know why she picked up his call. "So, are we on for dinner tonight or tomorrow?" asked Allen. "Ummmm….Tomorrow." "You can meet me at seven at Finley's," answered Morgan. "Cool, well, I hope the rest of your day turns out much better than how you sound," quizzed Allen. "Me too, I'll holla at you later," Morgan commented. Morgan kicked off her stilettos and fell back into her couch, once again peering up at the ceiling, with her eyes welling up with tears. Morgan thought to herself, "Why is everything going wrong right now?" "Why is everything going wrong, when I'm trying to do things right?" "I can't do this right now, I just can't!"

Before, she knew it, she had her phone in her hand and began texting Allen, "change of plans, meet me at Finley's tonight at eight." The random second thought act of choosing to meet Allen now, was something that she thought she needed to get her mind off of everything. Morgan got into the shower, let the steam relax her lungs and allowed the heat from the water to cascade down her entire body. She got out of the shower, wrapped her leopard print towel around her, and made her way to her closet to pick out the baddest dress and shoes. Morgan decided on a black dress with black and gold strapped stilettos. Just as she put her entire outfit out on the bed to make sure everything looked right, she realized that she never checked her phone to see if Allen even responded that he could meet her at Finley's tonight. His response was right on time, "See you at 8." Morgan walked passed her mirror and took one last look at herself, knowing that she looked ridiculously beautiful. Her dress fit her voluptuous frame perfectly and the hint of gold chunk jewelry just radiated against her chocolate skin tone. It had been a long time since she dressed up like this and she had to admit, it felt good.

She walked into Finley's and there he was right at the door waiting for her with a bouquet of white lilies in his hand. His stature, took her breath away. The suit coat, button up, and jeans he had on, made him look even more irresistible than he appeared in church. He had his locs done, pulled back away from his face, which exaggerated the structure of his cheekbones and allowed his caramel complexion to glow. He looked like the picture of perfection to her, although something in the back of her mind told her that he was far from perfect. "You look absolutely beautiful, these are for you" commented Allen. "Thank you, you don't look too bad yourself," joked Morgan. The waiter took to them to their seat and as he should, Allen pulled out the chair for her. Morgan was completely flattered. They ordered their food and had great conversation that night.

Allen explained that he was recently divorced from his wife of five years and that he had been attending Glory Mountain Baptist Church for a little over a year now on and off.

He stated that he worked in the information technology field. Morgan was truly enjoying their conversation. She couldn't tell if it was the three glasses of wine that she had inhaled or if it was him, but it was enjoyable and she was going to sit there and enjoy all of it! She explained that she was going through a transition period in her life and was helping to take care of her brother.

The waiter came to the table with their check and Morgan looked up to realize that she and Allen were the only two people left in the restaurant. "Wow, it looks like we overstayed our welcome," stated Allen. "I guess so," commented Morgan. After the waiter had left with Allen's credit card, he leaned across the table and sensually whispered, "I would love to continue our conversation tonight, I'm having too much fun to let this drop here." Morgan was surprised. "Where exactly did he think they were going to finish their conversation at?" she thought to herself. "Where are we going to do that at?" questioned Morgan. "We can figure that out as we get outta here," answered Allen slyly. They stood outside of Finley's talking and laughing for about another fifteen minutes. "Let's go back to my place and finish our conversation, I'm having such a good time and going around the corner to one of the bars, just isn't my scene," Allen explained. "Sure, but I'll follow you in my car," stated Morgan. "Deal, it's not very far from here," explained Allen.

Morgan got into her car and could not believe that she was agreeing to go back to Allen's place. She would never have done that before, but for some odd reason, she felt that Allen would be cool, since she had gotten to know him in church. Allen was right she thought, his apartment was only four blocks away from Finley's, he could have literally walked. She walked into Allen's apartment and checked everything out in the matter of seven seconds. "His place is too damn nice for a man to live here by himself," she thought to herself. 'Would you like another glass of wine," Allen questioned. "No, I'm good…I'll take some water though," stated Morgan, although she wanted to say yes.

Allen sat directly next to her on his couch, so close that she could smell his aftershave and his cologne all mixed together. She felt her heartbeat accelerating and began feeling flush. Morgan moved back slightly on the couch away from Allen, to make a slight distance between them both. "What's wrong," questioned Allen. "Nothing, I'm good," answered Morgan. With every vowel and consonant that lifted from Allen's mouth, Morgan could feel the heat of her inner desires becoming too hot to bear at that moment. He was intellectual, God fearing, sexy, and chivalrous, all of the right qualities. "Why is he single then," she thought to herself. "Allen, everything was so nice, but I gotta go," Morgan explained as she stood up. "You leaving already, the fun was just beginning," Allen smirked. "Yeah, sorry, but we can do this again," she commented. Just then like a magician performing his signature move, Allen's lips were wrapped around hers and his tongue was dancing slowly through her mouth. Her mind told her to push him away, but her arms held him tight and close to her. Before she knew it, her dress was making a statement on Allen's floor and they had managed to take over his bed. The strength of his hands felt so good moving up and down her thighs and the language that his tongue was speaking to her body sent shivers all over her body and just like that she gave in. Instantly, her thoughts had been replaced with the solitude of her feelings, leaving her thoughts to deal with the consequences of her actions when reality hit.

Buzzz....Buzzz...Buzzz.... Morgan jumped up and looked around. "Where am I she thought?" She looked over and seen Allen next to her knocked out. "My dress, where's my dress," she whispered to herself. "Where's my purse?" She looked at her phone and seen that it was 3:15 am and realized that it wasn't her phone ringing, but Allen's phone. She found her dress on the living room floor and her shoes in the bedroom. She hurried, got dress, and ran out the door. "I can't believe I did this," she blurted out once she sat down in her car. "Why me!" She started the car and sped off, in constant thought the entire time about what she did. Nothing about what her and Allen just shared sexually felt good in her spirit. She knew that she would now have to yet deal with something else on her plate, which was already full and spilling over with issues.

Morgan couldn't scrub her skin enough in the shower. She just felt so dirty and used after realizing that she had slept with Allen on their first date. She knew that he would probably think that she was easy and probably did this all the time with women. "Lakeya warned me about these church men." "Shit, their game is on some new level stuff," she thought to herself. Morgan may have been a stripper for most of her life, but the one thing that she wasn't, was a trick. She was selective who she chose to have sexual relationships with in the past and was usually very careful not to find herself in a situation like this.

She relaxed in her bed that night, with her towel still wrapped around her, numb to the truth that she placed herself in another sticky situation.

Chapter 10
NO DRAMA, LIKE CHURCH DRAMA

Morgan spent her entire Saturday in bed, rethinking over and over again, what she could have done that would have eliminated the situation that occurred. She wanted it to all be a dream, but the seven missed calls from Allen on her phone, was the realism that it was true. Knowing that she would have to face him again at church or bible study, Morgan selected his missed calls and let the phone rang. After going to his voicemail, she hung it. She was pissed at herself that she left her guard down with him and on the first date of all things. Truth be told, Morgan felt embarrassed and more and more like things were becoming beyond her reach in this new world that she had placed herself in. As she thought more and more, she took her sexual encounter with Allen as a sign that she was not fit to walk the straight and narrow path. Morgan entered the enigma of self-pity, fastly collapsing to the exact weight that she was trying to get her brother out of.

Morgan dozed off and awoke to her phone buzzing on her nightstand. Without looking to see who was calling, she answered the phone, "What's up?" "How are you beautiful?" Just then, Morgan realized that it was Allen on the other end. "Okay, but I could be better," Morgan explained. "Sorry about last night, I don't know what came over me…it was like it was meant to be," Allen expressed. "Wow, I really don't know what to say, I wasn't expecting any of that." "I really need some time to get my mind right Allen," Morgan commented. "I didn't mean to offend you Morgan, you are very beautiful you know." "I was overwhelmed by you," explained Allen. "Look Allen, I gotta go, I'll catch up with you later," Morgan insisted and hung up the phone. She knew right then and there that she had made a huge mistake by sleeping with him. If he seemed to have this great experience that he thought was okay and she felt as if the experience should have never happen, then something most definitely was not right. Regardless if something is right, you should never feel wrong and that is the truth that she was sticking with.

She never lifted herself out of bed, not even to eat. Morgan survived her Saturday with a sixty-four ounce bottle of water next to her bed, her cellphone, pillows, remote, and thoughts that played every game of pity patter on the devils playground.

Morgan woke up, looked at her phone and seen that it was Sunday all ready. She hopped out of the bed and ran to the bathroom. She had forgotten that she spent her entire Saturday in bed and didn't even get up to use the bathroom. Morgan looked at herself in the mirror and she looked rough. Her one eyelash was stuck to her eyebrow, remnants of her lipstick were still stained on her lips from Friday, and her hair looked a hot mess. "You gotta get it together," she said to herself in the mirror. She leaned in closer and glared at her reflection, not liking at all what she seen in the mirror. Morgan grabbed her facial cleanser, massaged it in her skin, and slowly walked into the shower.

After the shower, Morgan sat on the edge of her bed and debated about going to church. Although she normally didn't attend faithfully every Sunday, she felt like she really needed to go. Morgan didn't like the way she was feeling and couldn't deny it. She texted LaKeya, "let's do dinner or something after church. I need to talk."

"Ok," LaKeya texted.

As always, Morgan got to church late, just as the choir was ending their last selection and Rev. Shields was walking up the pulpit to preach. Rev. Shields urged everyone to stand for the reading of the word from Romans 12: 1-8. His sermon moved Morgan. He spoke on the power of God to transform you by renewing your mind, gave the steps of transformation, and then explained how God can use what the devil meant to hurt you with to bless you, by you using the gifts and talents that he has provided. That day for the very first time, Morgan felt as if Rev. Shields was talking directly to her and that he had been walking through her mind last night as she slept in sorrow. Morgan couldn't catch the tears fast enough from rolling down her face. As Rev. Shields directed everyone to stand and bow their heads for the Alter Call, Morgan found herself standing in the front of the alter releasing every last tear of hurt, transgression, fear, and pain, on the shoulders of one of the Deaconesses. As she was moved to a private room with the Deaconess, she was asked at the moment if she was ready to give her life to Christ. Without consolation, Morgan said, "Yes, I do."

Something just came over Morgan and she spilled every ounce of her spirit and gave it over to the Deaconess. The Deaconess looked at Morgan, smiled and said, "we all have stories baby, the power lies in our courage to tell them to help the next person find their way to the cross." "God has a special calling for you, the greater the calling, the greater the trials to get to your calling." The Deaconess provided her with a pamphlet regarding her walk with Christ and a listing of classes that she could take to understand her walk. Morgan felt as if she didn't need the classes and was learning all that she needed to know in Bible Study, but she liked the Deaconess and how calming she was, similar to Chaplin Carrington and thought that maybe she would attend.

Morgan could hear that church had ended and wanted to get to LaKeya before she walked out of church. As she made it to the church hallway, she looked around and didn't see her, so she decided to wait there until everyone exited. Just as she looked up, her eyes met Allen's. He instantly walked over to her and hugged her. "So good to see you, I seen you earlier in church, but thought you left out early." "No, I'm still here, waiting for my best friend," answered Morgan.

"Ohhh...didn't know your best friend went to church here," explained Allen. Morgan cut a half smile and began to look around for LaKeya, she wanted Allen to keep it movin', but he stood there next to her as if she welcomed his conversation. "There she is," Morgan happily exclaimed. She had never been so happy to see LaKeya. LaKeya walked towards Morgan with a weird look on her face, "Hey boo, you ready....I was lookin' for you." "Yup, let's be out," confirmed Morgan.

Morgan was excited to share with LaKeya her experience about giving her life to Christ and all about last night with Allen. Morgan was on a high that she had never experienced, she felt as if she couldn't contain her excitement any longer. As they were walking to the car, Morgan began explaining to LaKeya her excitement with giving her life to Christ and that the sermon delivered by the Reverend spoke to her spirit and situation in more ways than one. "Morgan, I am so happy for you," gleamed LaKeya. "I have prayed and prayed for you over the years and knew that God would save you," expressed LaKeya. "This deserves a celebration," LaKeya expressed. With a smile on her face like never before and a gleam in her eyes, Morgan could only say, "Thanks Keya." "So, you knew that you were going to give your life over when you texted me this morning," questioned LaKeya. "No, that was totally unexpected boo, totally!"

"It was about my date with the guy that I was telling you about from church, Allen." "He was standing right next to me, right when I saw you," explained Morgan. "I was so happy that you came when you did, because he was gettin' on my nerves being all clingy," Morgan further stated. Instantly, LaKeya pulled over and questioned, "the guy with the locs?" "Yeah, why," Morgan answered puzzled. "He told you his name is Allen?" "Anderson….Anderson Parker, the guy I've been cheatin' on Damian with." "What?" Morgan exclaimed. "Look Keya, I had no idea boo," Morgan stated. They both sat in LaKeya's car in silence for about fifteen minutes on South Street. LaKeya in tears, with her hand covering her eyebrows and Morgan staring in a daze. In all of their years as friends, they never ever thought they would have to deal with a situation like this. It was something from a movie or soap opera script, not something that happens in real life.

"Get out….Get out…GET OUT OF MY CAR!!!" LaKeya screamed. "Just get out." "Keya, c'mon we can work through this, he played us boo…he played us." "I told you, I had no idea…you never told me anything about him, other than you were cheating with this guy from your office." "How was I supposed to know," exclaimed Morgan with tears in her eyes.

"Just…get…out…of…my…. car," hissed LaKeya.

Morgan looked at her and had never seen her look the way that she did. She pulled her purse to her shoulder, opened the car door, slowly got out and as quick as her left foot hit the sidewalk and the door closed, LaKeya took off, leaving nothing behind except the stale memories of the moment that just erupted before their very eyes. "I can't believe this," "How did this happen." Morgan thought to herself. With anger in her spirit and tears forming in her eyes, she began walking back to her car at the church. That walk, felt like the longest walk, with three inch heels on and a heart as heavy as a ton of bricks sitting on her shoulders. As soon as she made it back to her car and sat down, she pulled her shoes off and threw them in the back of her car. Morgan was stunned and emotional. In all of her days as a stripper, dabbling in and out of drugs, and being in the environment that she had been in, the possibility of something like this greeting her at the front door, puzzled her.. and of all days for this to happen, it had to happen on what was to be one of the most memorable and happiest days of her life, the day that she gave her life to Christ.

She didn't know what to make of the entire situation and was hoping that LaKeya wasn't putting blame on her and that she was going to allow this to come between their friendship. Morgan called LaKeya four times and she didn't pick up. That was not like LaKeya at all. "I just don't know what to do," she voiced out loud. "God why...why this too...it seems that everything in my life is just filling with hurt and disappointment…what's the use…what's the use when it appears that I'm losing a grip on everything in my life…..why would you bring me here…why me…what do I have that you want…what…what is it….just take it…just take it Lord…take it," she proclaimed to the Lord on her knees in the middle of her kitchen laying prostrate. With nothing to lose, Morgan surrendered. She was tired and threw in the towel. She made up her mind that if she was going to make a change, she was going to do so wholeheartedly and go hard!

During this transition period, she had been so worried about everyone else and making sure that they were stabilized, not focusing the time that she needed on doing the same for herself. She knew then and there that she had to get herself together first, before she could be of assistance to anyone else in her life. Morgan knew that it was time to put all of her energy into her.

Chapter 11
HE WORKS IN MYSTERIOUS WAYS

The next morning was sure to be the true test of whether or not Morgan could make it through the rest of her newfound life. She awoke motivated. Motivated to get it right. Motivated to make moves. Motivated to do something. It was Monday, her day to check on Maurice. She was dreading walking into his condition today, but knew that if she had to at the very least pop in. Morgan realized that she never called Deuce to find out what really happened between him and her brother.

"Hey Deuce, this is Morgan…Reece's sister." "What's good?" he questioned. "Look, I know it's not my business and Reece is gonna kill me for this, but what happened, my brother is in a bad spot and I need to know," she explained. "Ask him…he cut it off…as he see's it…I'm the reason why he's in the condition that he is in." "I mean what can I say….I bounced…I don't have time for that soft shit," expressed Deuce. "He knows what it is and I got too much goin' on in my life to sit there and have someone pointin' the finger at me," Deuce explained. "I know you ain't mean no harm and I won't kill your vibe with brother, I moved on and I hope he gets his shit together," expressed Deuce. "Aiight, thanks Deuce, I feel you," stated Morgan. "It ain't about nothin'," stated Deuce. Morgan had an ounce of hope that it was something that she could do to get Deuce back in her brother's life, thinking that it would improve his feelings and help her out a bit from being the only one dealing with him and his volatile nature.

Searching through her phone for the websites to the two nursing facilities that Chaplin Carrington told her about, Morgan was optimistic about what they were hiring for. The one facility had a job as a caretaker that she thought she may like to do. The description was the same thing that she had been doing with Maurice, so she thought, how much harder could it be to do this for someone else and actually get paid. After applying for the job online, she felt a sign of relief. Even if she did not receive a call back, she knew that she made an important step in the right direction.

She looked over the pamphlet that the Deaconess gave her in church about her new member classes and her walk with Christ. She noticed that her classes were actually the same time as Bible Study. Morgan was upset, because she loved the teachings that she was receiving in

Bible Study and hated to miss it, but realized that going to the new member classes would probably help her out as well. Morgan understood that she had to get over her impulsive nature and recognize that most of her life's situations have been led by her being impulsive and rushing into situations that she found herself trapped in and motionless for years. Her running away from home, being in a past abusive relationship, stripping, and finally the sexual encounter with Allen, which had now transpired to severing a relationship with her best friend. Thinking of all of this left Morgan feeling down and discouraged, but in the back of her mind, she knew that it would not always be like this. She got herself together and made her way over to Maurice's. "Lord please help me and please help my brother get through this," she prayed as she closed her front door.

It was starting to drizzle, as Morgan stood at the entrance of Maurice's apartment complex. She realized that her umbrella was in the car and she didn't want to mess her hair up, so she sprinted across the parking lot and jumped into the car. "Thank God, Maurice was in a much better spirit today," she thought to herself. He didn't talk to her much, but at least he didn't insult her as usual. Buzzz….Buzz…Buzzz…just as she went to plug her phone into the car charger, it started to ring with an unknown number showing. "Hello" "Hi, may I please speak to Morgan Sullivan?" "Yeah, this is me…who is this?" "Hi, my name is Alicia and I'm calling from The Nurses Touch, would you be available to come in for an interview on Friday at 9:45 am or next Tuesday at 8:00 am for the mobile caretaker position?" "Yes, I can come in on Friday morning, thank you," commented Morgan. "Great, we'll see you then." Morgan was excited; she couldn't believe that they actually called her back. She did not have any prior job experience to list on her application and could not understand how she was selected to come in for the interview. Regardless, that call placed her on cloud nine, ten and eleven. For once, something was working in her favor and she enjoyed how it felt.

Morgan knew she was showin' off! She arrived at new members class on time, to the point that she was the only one there. Morgan pulled out her brochure to make sure that she was in the right classroom on the right day, which she was. A few minutes later, the Deaconess came walking in that ministered to her, but no one else. "Hi there, so glad to see you, I don't believe I shared with you fully, I'm Deaconess Gibson." "Hi, where is everybody else?" "I'm not sure, but we'll give them two more minutes and then I'm going to get started."

"Okay, I hope they show up," Morgan commented. She didn't want to be the only one in the class, it felt weird, being just her and Deaconess Gibson. "Well, let's get started," cheered Deaconess Gibson and so on went the first class, just them two. Deaconess Gibson shared about the history of the church, its mission and vision, discovering gifts and talents, and the ministries that were available in the church. It was a lot of information to take in and Morgan was all ears, taking notes and everything. "I like that it's just us, it's more intimate and we can get down to the meat and bones of things," shared Deaconess Gibson. "Yeah, it's cool, I wasn't sure how it would go, but I have to admit that I like it as well," expressed Morgan. "So how do you know what your gifts and talents are and what ministries you should be in?" questioned Morgan. "You are right on target, here, complete this questionnaire in the book and bring it back to class next week." "Take your time completing it and try not to rush, it will help determine what your gifts and talents are, as well as explain several examples of gifts and talents and that is how we determine which ministries for you to become involved in," thoroughly explained Deaconess Gibson. "Okay, I can do that…THANK YOU," Morgan expressed. Morgan fingered through the workbook that Deaconess Gibson gave her to complete and made her way out of the building. She actually enjoyed the class and was glad that she went.

Friday rolled around so fast. Morgan walked out of her interview feeling as if she could have done better. She couldn't believe that the job only paid $10.75 an hour, but it was better than nothing and especially for somebody that had literally no job experience in that field, only the experience of taking care of her brother. She hoped that she got the job and could actually have something constructive to do with her time during the day. Things were really looking up for her in some areas and she was proud of her progress this week. Morgan pulled her phone out of her purse and seen that she had four missed calls. Two from LaKeya, one from Allen, and one from Fat Kat. "Really," she blurted out loud. Each of those calls had drama written all over it. To call or not to call was the ambivalent question that Morgan pondered on from The Nurses Touch to her home. Just when things were gettin' good, here were issues and conflict right around the corner waiting. So much for good times, Morgan thought.

Her first call went to LaKeya. "Hey Keya, you called…how are you?" "Not good, look, I just called to apologize about the other day, I'm sorry." "I'm just in a bad place right now, I broke down and confessed to Damian and….and…..he took Joy and left Morgan…he left me….," LaKeya cried. "Keya, I am so sorry to hear that, I'm sure it was just a gut reaction for him….did the both of you have a chance to talk further yet…what about counseling?" Morgan quizzed. "Every time I bring it up, he cuts me off and just talks about Joy…he's filing for full custody…and this is all my fault…every last piece of it," LaKeya explained. "Oh man…Keya, have you talked to anyone else," Morgan questioned. "No, no one, I'm so ashamed… I let everyone down, especially Joy," expressed LaKeya. "I'm lost, Anderson….Allen or whatever he calls himself, won't even return my phone calls after I confronted him about dating me and you at the same time," she explained. "Girl, he had the nerve to say that he was not my man and had no idea that you were my friend, so I had no reason to be mad at him." "Is he serious?" LaKeya demanded. "Keya, worrying about him is the last thing that should be on your mind, you gotta focus on gettin' your family back, it is most definitely not supposed to be like this at all," shared Morgan. "I'll keep y'all in my prayers, I don't know what more to say," Morgan explained. "I don't know what to do and I don't know where to go...I'm ashamed to tell my parents," shared LaKeya. "Well, they're gonna find out one day and it would be best coming from you," Morgan suggested. Morgan wanted to offer to go to LaKeya's parents house with her, but knew that if she did that, she would easily fall back into allowing the issues of others to overshadow the issues in her life that she needed to be working on. Although she missed LaKeya being around, Morgan knew that all of the drama in her life was brought about because of the issues that she brought into her home and the only person that could work on fixing that was LaKeya. It hurt to see her like this, but something in her spirit just moved her to remove herself from the situation. "Call me later Keya and let me know how it went and how you are doing, you know I love you boo," expressed Morgan. "Love you too," LaKeya whispered as Morgan hung up the phone. Morgan made up her mind that she was not calling Allen or Fat Kat back, they were both two individuals that she wanted to leave in her past.

Morgan didn't even feel her phone ringing, but seen the screen showing an incoming call from a random number. She almost didn't answer it, but picked up. "Hello" "Hi, may I please speak with Morgan Sullivan?" "This is Morgan." "Morgan, this is Alicia from The Nurses Touch and I would like to offer you the mobile caretaker position." "Yes…yes, I will take it." "Great, can you come in next Tuesday for orientation and we'll get you started?" "Yes, that will work for me, I'll see you then." Morgan did the happy dance all the way through the threshold of her house. Excited was an understatement. She couldn't wait to tell Deaconess Gibson. They're relationship had grown. Morgan began looking to Deaconess Gibson as a mother figure.

Morgan was coming up on her third new member class and was eager to find out her gifts and talents. She told Deaconess Gibson about her new job and some of the conflicting issues she was having in her past. Morgan felt inclined in the moment to share with her that she once was a stripper, her issues with abandonment from her parents, and the things she had experienced and seen in her life as a stripper. The Deaconess quietly comforted her and explained, "we ALL have a past my dear…trust me." "Some may act as if they do not, but we all do and the only reason we are here in the present and future, is because of Gods saving grace and mercy," Deaconess Gibson explained. Morgan just smiled in embarrassment. "There is nothing to be ashamed of, nothing at all," Deaconess Gibson further expressed. "Now let's talk about your gifts and talents report." "You scored very high in Evangelism, Helps/Service, and Leadership." "So what does all of that mean?" questioned Morgan. "It means that you are great at helping people and have a gift for sharing the word of God, something similar to a preacher," Deaconess Gibson explained. "We'll talk about putting them to practice and where you can use them here next week." "I want you to start keeping a daily journal, something like a diary, to write down your daily thoughts and feelings." "I have an idea, but we'll talk more about that later,"

Deaconess Gibson exclaimed. Morgan left new membership class in another great mood. She could not believe that she scored high in sharing the word of God, she really did not think that would be a gift of hers, apparently she was wrong. She was still on the fence about it, but had other things to think about, like her first day of work.

Morgan's first day at The Nurses Touch went well. "Sheesh...every last piece of paper up in here you have to sign," she commented to herself. Filing out all of the paperwork was tiring. "I see why I worked under the table for so long," she thought to herself. Four hours later, she was finally leaving The Nurses Touch, ready to start working with her first client in a few days. She could not believe that she had a real tax paying job and that it was only paying $10.75 an hour. Eleven months ago, no one could have made her believe that she would have been in this place in her life. "It's funny how someone else's situation can actually turn your situation around," Morgan thought to herself.

Chapter 12
TO THE PULPIT

The opportunities of life were finally greeting Morgan with open hands and welcomed opportunities. Life wasn't perfect and without problems, but it surely beat waking up most of time hung-over, with a deep rooted hate for yourself, and a numbness to life. She was living for the first time and not merely existing and it felt good!

She didn't know how she would like going into different homes and taking care of people, but how hard could it be, if she used to walk around naked for the most part allowing men to touch every part of her body. This at the very least had to be easy. For the most part, she had fairly good experiences with her three clients. Cooking, cleaning, taking them shopping and doing other odds and ends with them, was actually refreshing. Some days they got on her nerves and others, she enjoyed them, especially their stories filled with wisdom. Morgan had been working so many hours that she lost focus of her faith walk. Her church attendance on Sunday was still sporadic, but she had missed her new member class with Deaconess Gibson and felt guilty. She knew that she had to work on scheduling and setting time frames to get everything into her life, which was a completely new outlook on life. Finally, she had the chance to call Deaconess Gibson and re-schedule to meet the following Thursday evening for her final class.

As usual, Morgan started class off sharing her experiences at work , with her brother, and the inner turmoil that she had been experiencing. Deaconess Gibson was happy to hear that she was staying on task with the other situations of life and that Morgan was taking the time to journal her daily thoughts as she was going through this process. "I brought my journal, in case you want to see it," exclaimed Morgan. "I've been doing exactly what you told me to do and it feels good to let everything out at the end of the day," expressed Morgan. "Great, but I don't need to see it, that exercise was for you." "I noticed that you kept so many things on the inside and rarely opened up to anyone about what's really going on inside of you," explained Deaconess Gibson.

"You have a powerful story Morgan, have you ever thought of sharing it, something like a testimony?" questioned Deaconess Gibson. "Sharing it where…in front of the entire church?" "I don't know about that?" expressed Morgan as she scrunched her eyebrows up. "I look at you and see the glory of God all over you." "Have you ever taken some time to think, that you could've easily not been here…you could've easily managed to find yourself trapped in your lifestyle and motionless…but you are not…you are here." "He brought you here for a reason…there's always someone out there that needs to understand the true transformation power of Christ," Deaconess Gibson explained gleefully. Morgan was speechless. She had never stood up in front of anyone and spoken to them about anything and she sure as heck wasn't planning on doing it in front of the entire congregation and tell people her business. Deaconess Gibson was trippin' for sure Morgan thought. "You pray on it sweetie." "We're having a special service on the last Friday of the month that involves others sharing their stories and I know that yours would truly bless all ears that it falls upon," begged Deaconess Gibson. Smiling, but unsure, Morgan agreed to think about it, although her thoughts were that it was a definite NO! Deaconess Gibson moved in and hugged Morgan and whispered, "It's not about being perfect, that's HIS job." "Be blessed Morgan."

Morgan got into her car and looked into the rearview mirror thinking "Deaconess Gibson has no idea." As she was pulling out the parking lot, she happened to see Allen walking one of the women from church to her car. Morgan just shook her head. Although she had gotten caught up for a second with Allen, she knew that the actions that transpired immediately afterwards, had everything to do with God. She knew for a fact that she was blessed and that God had saved her for a reason, but to share her story, really didn't sound reasonable. As Deaconess Gibson advised, Morgan prayed about it that night amongst other things.

Getting up early and preparing for work was becoming common place for Morgan, even on her days off. Morgan arose Tuesday morning with Maurice on her mind. Since she had been working, she didn't have time to check on him but more than once a week and when she got there, he was usually pretending to be in a good mood. She opened the door to Maurice's apartment and began calling his name, but there was no response. Morgan looked all over his apartment, but couldn't find him, until she walked completely into his room and looked behind the door. She couldn't believe what she saw. Her hands began to tremble and her heart dropped to the floor. There was her Maurice hanging there from his pull up bar on a rope…dead. Morgan burst into tears, calling Maurice's name and screaming, "NO," as loud as she could. She fumbled through her purse and called 9-1-1. Numb, frozen, and in shock she dropped to her knees at the door and waited for help to come. Nothing in life could have ever prepared her for this. Not Maurice, not her rock, her only blood in this world. "Not him….not him….not him…" she loudly sulked into the arms of the officer that arrived on the scene. He calmly took her information and ensured that she made it home safe.

Morgan was a zombie, she could not believe that Maurice had taken his own life. She felt horrible, thinking over and over again about the days that she missed seeing him and how she could have fit in a little bit of time to make it to check in on him. Morgan was the lowest that she had ever felt in her life and felt that life as she thought she knew it was now over.

Unknowingly, she called the only person that would know what she needed to do, Deaconess Gibson, sharing every gritty detail of how she found Maurice. Deaconess Gibson advised Morgan that she would meet her at her home in the next hour and assist with the funeral services. Morgan turned on the TV to silence her thoughts and that fast, coverage of Maurice's death was blaring across the news. "Nooooooooooooo," she screamed, allowing the tears to overcome her face. Just then, she heard the doorbell. She opened the door and Deaconess Gibson was standing there, with open arms. Morgan fell into her arms and cried a river. Deaconess Gibson slowly walked her inside and just held her, slowly rubbing her back. Morgan was broken, but relieved to have the spiritual advice of Deaconess Gibson. Deaconess Gibson took Morgan's hand in hers, looked her in the eyes and expressed, "I am so sorry for your loss my dear…..God will see you through this." "I'm going to make you some tea, drink it and get some rest," she explained. Morgan drank the tea and instantly, she was asleep.

Morgan awoke and jumped up from her couch. "Maurice," she yelled. Yesterday felt like a dream, until she reached for her phone and had forty missed calls. She knew at that moment that it was true. As promised, Deaconess Gibson helped her see her way through the funeral process. Morgan knew that she would have never been able to make it without the guidance and prayer of Deaconess Gibson. Morgan decided to have Maurice's body cremated and have a small intimate funeral service for him, due to her limited funds. In attendance was only her, LaKeya, Deuce, and Deaconess Gibson. She didn't know how she did it, but she managed to go to work the week following the funeral and keep moving. The main thing that she remembered that Deaconess Gibson told her was to take her time grieving and to not allow anyone to rush her. Most days she felt guilty for not checking on him as much. Every day since the service, Morgan visited Maurice and apologized for not being there for him, but today, she spoke to him about Deaconess Gibson and her wanting her to share her story. "What should I do Reece?" "I just don't know…I prayed about it…but I can't stop my mind from thinking about you." "I miss you Reece…your laughter, your corny jokes, and even your attitude," "I would have given anything to take your pain away, I honestly didn't know you were hurting that bad…I will never ever forget you big brah…you will always be my hero," Morgan sadly expressed.

Morgan slid on her Gucci shades and exited the Mausoleum, when she walked past a woman that looked just like Sugar. Just as she passed her, Morgan turned and called her name, "Sugar" and woman slowed down her pace, but kept moving. "It's Mystery." "The woman turned around and Morgan removed her shades and could see clearly that it was her. They both walked towards each other and hugged. "What are you doing here?" "What are you doing here?" They both laughed. "I work here, helping families find the locations for their loved ones final resting place, but my real name is Carmen" shared Sugar. "Well, hey Carmen, you look great." "My brother passed away last week and this is his final resting place, I was visiting him," explained Morgan. "So very sorry for your loss, I know how much he meant to you," expressed Carmen. "I'm so happy to see that you left Top Shelf and that you are doin' your thang,"

Morgan commented. "Once you left and I saw you of all people could do it, I knew that I could too…I just made my plan, set my mind and found my way out." "It's not the money that I'm used to, but the peace of mind is priceless," Carmen shared. "Wow, you got that right, I know exactly what you're talkin' about," Morgan commented. "Look, here is my card, don't lose it, we have to get together when we have time, I'm scheduled to meet with a family at this plot down here in five minutes," stated Carmen and that fast she was gone, walking down the corridor. In that moment, Morgan knew that it was God and Maurice sending her a sign that she needed to share her story at the Friday night service that Deaconess Gibson invited her to.

When she got home, Morgan pulled out her two journals and began paging through them, feverishly looking for things to say at the service.

It was only one day away, which left little time to get everything together. Morgan held her journals tight against her chest and prayed to God for his blessing over the words that she was preparing to share on Friday night. She opened her new notebook and wrote and wrote and wrote, until she crafted her story and her message. Morgan didn't know how long or how short she needed to be, but seven journal pages later, front and back, she was done.

Morgan arrived to church, parked her car, and sat in the parking lot watching everyone go in. From the looks of it, she could sense that a majority of the people going in were about her age or a few years older. "Deaconess Gibson tried to set me up," Morgan thought to herself. She never fully confirmed or agreed to attend to Deaconess Gibson, so she could drive off and go back to the comforts of her home. Morgan looked in her rearview mirror and glared at herself. She knew that she had to do this, but needed help erasing her fear. Just as she put her head down, there was a tap on her window from none other than Deaconess Gibson. "Morgan, you decided to come." "I hope you will share your magnificent story," she commented. "I will Deaconess Gibson....I will," Morgan confessed.

After one of the Deacons opened up the event with prayer and everyone joined in with song, it was time for sharing. The Deacon spoke briefly about trials and tribulations and how they can often times be placed in our lives to make us slow down and look into our own lives to see what changes we have to make, so that we can grow from them. The moment that Morgan was ready to get over with and at the same time, hoping that there was not enough time for, arose. The Deacon announced that there was a member that had a very special testimony to share about God's true power of transformation.

With everyone clapping, Morgan slowly made her way to pulpit and looked over the crowd to realize that nearly fifty to fifty-five people were in the service. Her nerves were in overdrive. Her palms were sweating and her legs were shaking. Just as she was about to make her way off the stage, she felt a hand on her back and could sense that it was Deaconess Gibson by the smell of her perfume. "You can do this, I am sitting right behind you."

Softly Morgan whispered, "This is for you Maurice." "Hi, my name is Morgan, but I used to be known as Mystery. "For a little over eleven years, I spent my life as a stripper…allowing men and sometimes women to do unspeakable things to me for their pleasures." "I left home at the age of sixteen thinking that I was in love and found myself in an abusive relationship and because of fleeing from that relationship with nowhere to go and no money, I was left with no other choice than to strip to earn my money. "I have been in the roughest of situations and abused drugs and alcohol, but Glory be to God…I am here." At that moment, everyone clapped and you could hear "amen's" dancing all over the church. She continued on to share her story of abandonment from her parents, her relationship with her brother, her newfound employment and goals, and the fact that her brother's illness and death were the trials in her life that focused her and ultimately led her to the cross.

"As the Bible states in 2 Corinthians 5:17, Therefore, if any man be in Christ, he is a new creature; old things are passed away; behold, all things have become anew." "So ladies and gentlemen, this is my true story of how I have made it *From The Pole To The Pulpit*, stay tuned, because I am sure that there will be plenty more to add to my story if our God has anything to do with it!"

With tears in her eyes, Morgan looked up from her journal and could see every single person in the sanctuary on their feet clapping, waving their hands and giving high praises to God. She stood there amazed, watching as person after person made their way to the alter looking to either be saved or have hands lain upon. In that moment at that time, Morgan finally knew exactly what God had called her to do and she made a vow to do it, with nothing other than excellence.

Regardless of where we are in our lives as women, each of us share similar stories. It's just that some of us are too proud, too ashamed, too stuck, too careless, or too self centered to share our truths, leaving us in an abyss of powerlessness. Our daughters, nieces, cousins and future strongholds are left to question their very existence in this complex and bias-centered world, because we chose to remain voiceless. What's the use of our freedom and tongues, if we're going to do nothing more than taste what is familiar?

There is much in life that we have to offer as women, so why don't we? Why do we hold onto the very things that made us into who we are today, without sharing them? Even if they happen to be failures, I'm positive that something was gained.

It's time that we fellowship about more than the latest television show, community rumor, or video. Whatever your story is, I challenge you to tell it! Tell it privately, publicly, intimately, and/or openly. Remove the selfish veil and think about who might need that story, just to believe enough to make it another day.

Peace and Blessings,

Edquina

ABOUT THE AUTHOR

Edquina Washington is a Community Relations professional with a passion for building thriving communities through the arts and social justice. Her heart is empowering women to build one another through sharing their stories. She enjoys being involved in the political arena and working on projects that push the envelope and promote community growth.

Edquina is a lover of the arts and the intrinsic value that it adds to a community. She is a poet, performer and the founder of Liberated Sista, a blog dedicated to inspire and create dialogue about the world around her.

Edquina holds a Bachelor of Science in Criminal Justice from York College and a Masters of Human Services in Social and Community Services from Capella University. She resides in York, PA with her three children.

Made in the USA
Middletown, DE
26 May 2019